Dear Diary,

Uncle Roth and Melba kissed today! I've been trying to push them together, but I didn't think Uncle Roth would ever stop dating those snooty models. Melba didn't like the way they always put me down, and I think she talked to Uncle Roth about it. Melba always tries to look out for me. I'm glad she's my nurse. She's loads of fun and really nice. And even though she and Uncle Roth are insisting they are only friends, I think there's something special between them....

Got to run!

Adriane

Please address questions and book requests to: Silhouette Reader Service
U.S.: 3010 Walden Ave., P.O. Box 1325, Buffalo, NY 14269
Canadian: P.O. Box 609, Fort Erie, Ont. L2A 5X3

SOUTH CAROLINA

LAURIE PAIGE

The Sea at Dawn

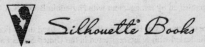

Published by Silhouette Books

America's Publisher of Contemporary Romance

SILHOUETTE BOOKS
300 East 42nd St.,
New York, N.Y. 10017

ISBN 0-373-47190-4

THE SEA AT DAWN

Copyright © 1995 by Olivia M. Hall

Printed in U.S.A.

Dear Reader,

I often find, when I write a book, that the story is a combination of events that happened to me or friends. This story was like that—a visit to friends in South Carolina and a twilight walk through the ruins of an old plantation ensnared me right away. I knew I had to do a story in this setting. It was as simple and as compelling as that.

The other element, the teenage girl trying to live up to an image of herself that didn't match her personality, came from an article in a magazine about a teenager who tried to live up to her father's expectations that she make perfect grades and her mother's expectations that she be one of the most popular girls in school. With such unconscious but high demands on her, the girl felt constantly on the verge of failure, no matter how high her grades or how well she performed as a cheerleader. It was only after therapy sessions that the parents realized they mentioned their own successes in school each time she made the honor roll or landed a lead in the school play, thus conveying that they expected the daughter to do as well. She thought she had to do better.

The friend who gave me the tour of the plantation had been a nurse. So there it was—all the background elements I needed. Add one good-looking bachelor uncle, parents who were on the verge of divorce, a teenager who needed security and self-esteem, plop them into a fascinating, romantic environment, then throw in one heroine to stir it all together and add her own complications and *voilà!* the story was ready to be written....

Laurie Paige

Chapter One

Melba Holly gripped the chromium railing of the pool steps and pulled herself onto the patio, water droplets spraying outward in a circle around the two wet imprints of her feet. Leaning forward, she finger-combed her hair over one shoulder and then wrung out the excess water before giving it a toss to send it cascading down her back. The dark caramel coloring had lightened to gold and amber tones from the hours she had spent in the sun during the two and a half weeks she had been at Webster Island, South Carolina.

Today was Friday, the beginning of her third weekend in this semitropical paradise, and she still couldn't believe she was here. She glanced around at the pool, the patio and surrounding gardens, and the tri-level Spanish-style house with a shake of her head. A Garden of Eden, she mused.

With a pleased sense of surprise, she realized that

she felt contented, as if she had been renewed in spirit. She searched through her memories as one would explore the scars from an old wound and found that they were painless. Time does heal, she thought. It was a matter of perspective...and acceptance. A person had to learn to accept the things that couldn't be changed. This was what she wanted Adriane to learn.

As a self-employed psychiatric nurse working out of a medical clinic in Charleston, she usually dealt with routine illnesses, but this time her client was eighteen-year-old Adriane Langdon, whose physical condition would hardly qualify her as a typical patient in any sense of the word. Melba had been asked to take the case by Dr. Scott, who was the founder of the clinic as well as a personal friend of the Langdon family.

The young girl had been brought to the clinic three months ago, pale and thin, her physical resources nearly exhausted as she fought off yet another bout of flu. The past year had been impossibly hard on the teenager, and her body had rebelled from the stresses put on it. The combination of poor diet and little sleep had taken their toll. Now she was much better, having recovered her health and all but ten pounds of her original weight. What was more important, she and her mother had come to understand the problems that had led to Adriane's rundown condition.

Mrs. Langdon, a notable beauty, had been the star of her own debutante season before her marriage to the son of an old Charlestonian family. She had expected the same of her daughter, without allowing for differences in their personalities. The endless parties, the nerve-wracking knowledge of always being on display, as well as the stress of her final year in high school, had simply been too much for Adriane. The effort to be like her mother, to be constantly poised and glamorous, had been an impossible task.

The situation was complicated by the fact that her parents had split up during the past year. The failure of her parents' marriage coupled with her own imagined shortcomings had overtaxed her physical and emotional reserves.

At Dr. Scott's request, Melba had agreed to spend two months with Adriane and had driven her patient and herself down to Webster Island while Mrs. Langdon had stayed in Charleston to take care of some legal business before joining them later in the month.

A smile glinted in Melba's gray-green eyes as she remembered the beautiful drive from the city over to Hilton Head Island, ending at a luxurious resort called Sea Point, which was on the southern tip of the island near the famous Sea Pines Plantation. The two of them had taken a boat from the resort to this small, private island.

Both the resort and Webster Island were owned by Adriane's uncle, Roth Webster. Briefly, Melba wondered where he was and why he didn't live in his own house on his island, before her thoughts went back to her patient.

Adriane had chattered the whole way from the city to the island. Usually, Melba's patients were much older and sicker than the bouncy young girl.

As a nurse, she had always made herself unobtrusive in a household, going quietly about the business of regulating the sick person's day. But this situation was different. From the first, Adriane had treated her as a trusted friend, confiding the secrets and worries that were hidden behind the saucy facade until Melba imagined she knew the girl better than she knew herself.

From the conversation, Melba knew that Adriane's mother, Glenna Langdon, thought her brother Roth was an incorrigible playboy, but Adriane considered him an indulgent uncle. That didn't necessarily indicate a split personality—a person could be different things to different people. Still, Roth Webster sounded like something of an enigma.

"Mother's turned into a prude in her old age." Adriane had defended her male relative. "He's really wonderful. And only thirty-two." She had given Melba a sly glance from her hazel eyes. "Maybe you'll fall in love with him."

"I doubt it," she had replied dryly.

Adriane had wormed the facts of Melba's tragic first love out of her while at the duplex apartment where Melba was packing for the trip. The teenager had returned the confidence by speaking of her uncle's love life. "I was afraid last year that he was going to marry Shirl Bard."

The way she said the name meant it should have some significance to Melba. "Who's Shirl Bard?" she'd dutifully asked.

Adriane had been amazed. "The highest paid photographer's model in history!"

Melba had suppressed her disgust with the uncle.

No wonder Adriane had doubts about her own self-image if that was the type of female her beloved Uncle Roth went for. Between them, her mother and uncle had inadvertently fostered in Adriane the notion that she had to be just as glamorous in order to be loved.

"She must be pretty," Melba had said in a non-committal tone, to show that she wasn't impressed.

"She's snooty," Adriane had decided after thinking it over. "I think she got mad because Uncle Roth wouldn't be ordered around. Men don't like bossy women," she'd stated matter-of-factly. "He would make a perfect husband, though. Really, I'm not kidding!" she had protested when Melba started laughing.

"Would you mind terribly if I found my own husband? It's kind of you to be concerned, but honestly, Adriane, I can manage on my own."

"You haven't so far," the irrepressible teenager had reminded her.

A resolute determination pushed the smile out of the sea-green eyes. Melba had felt out of place when she first arrived in this wealthy Eden, but now her protective instincts were aroused. Life was complicated enough for the youngster in her charge without hassles from feuding relatives adding to the turmoil.

An ache invaded her chest, reminding her of the emotional scars from her own past and the two children she and her fiancé had planned to have before the accident had ended that idea. She wondered if one of the reasons she identified so much with Adriane was because of her own painful experiences in which she had had to learn to accept those things she couldn't change.

Vowing to do whatever was necessary to shield her patient from further hurt at this fragile stage in her life, she turned toward the grassy lawn bordering the patio. Her thoughts were diverted to the present when Hattie, the cook and housekeeper, came out of the kitchen and up to the level where Melba had paused to fluff her hair in the drying rays of the sun.

The housekeeper was a tall, buxom woman with totally white hair that was permed into a ruff of soft curls that started over her temples and wreathed the back of her head just above her collar. Her voice was rather high and thin so that when she laughed, it sounded more like a quiet cackle than laughter. She and Melba were already good friends, drawn together by mutual concern for Adriane.

"Would you like a snack now and a late dinner tonight?" she asked. "Or would you rather have dinner early and the snack at bedtime?" She left the choice up to the nurse.

Melba considered the options. She had eaten a substantial lunch and so had Adriane, but hunger pangs told her that a snack might be called for. Then another idea came to her. Last Friday, the three of them had gone over to Sea Point for dinner. The seafood buffet, a casual affair served out on the patio, had been delicious. Also, she thought it was good for the teenager to get out and mingle with other people besides herself and Hattie.

She answered the housekeeper's question with one of her own. "How do you feel about going over to the resort for dinner?"

"Fine with me," Hattie said.

"Then let's go over to Sea Point early and catch the buffet when it first starts. I think Adriane and I can hold out another hour or so before eating."

"There are fresh cookies in the kitchen," Hattie advised. She was one of those rare persons who could be motherly toward other people and yet let them make decisions in their areas of expertise, as she did regarding the eating schedule for Adriane.

"I'll wait," Melba decided, giving Hattie a warm smile as the cook-housekeeper started down the short flight of steps to return to the kitchen.

Alone again, Melba wondered what was keeping Adriane. She had climbed out of the pool and gone around the side of the house looking for the beach ball, tossing a challenge over her shoulder to Melba for a game of basketball in the pool. The two of them had gone over to Sea Point nearly every day to play tennis, making up a foursome with a young man Adriane had met and with anybody else they could find—usually the resort pro—for Melba's partner. Adriane had looked over the men at the resort with an eye toward possible escorts for her nurse but found them too old or too young, too worldly or already taken.

"If only Uncle Roth would come," Adriane had moaned.

Smiling to herself, Melba glanced around again. Sand dunes and pine trees, a grassy quadrangle, pleasant shade created by the roof extending from the house, Hattie to cook and care for them, a riot of spring blossoms—azaleas, forsythia, butter-cups—so much beauty that it grabbed one's breath away and squeezed the heart into a lump of pulsing sensations. This truly was paradise...even without the wonderful Uncle Roth!

Hearing footsteps, she smiled as Adriane came across the patio carrying a wreath of snowdrops in one hand and wearing another on her head. Affection for the girl surged through Melba. Every day she felt closer to Adriane.

"Here, I made you a crown, too." The girl brought the offering and placed it on Melba's head. "Oh, look!" she exclaimed, catching sight of their twin images in the panes of the open French doors. "Aren't we pretty?" She straightened her crown of flowers.

"Yes, we are," Melba agreed, then added casually, "but I've always felt pretty. My grandmother told me that we were born with the looks God gave us, but by the time we're forty, we have nobody to blame but ourselves if we're displeased with them."

"What did she mean?"

"That our personality changes our looks to the type of person we really are. If you're a sourpuss, you look like one!" There was nothing sour about the laughing faces reflected in the glass. A slender brow arched over the sea-green eyes. "Maybe we wouldn't do as models for Greek sculpture," Melba continued, "but we could pose for any advertisements needing lively, bright, healthy, cheerful, audacious, stubborn females. We'd even wear clothes if they wanted us to." Her face was solemn as she stated this last bit. Melba and Adriane dispensed with their bathing suits while on the private island;

Melba felt it was one way to help Adriane be more comfortable with her body and her looks.

Adriane was laughing aloud before the list was completed. She tilted her head to study the two images that were within an inch of the same height, comparing her own hazel eyes with the gray-green ones, the streaky-blond hair with the golden amber locks, her slender oval face with the delicately rounded one.

"We could be sisters," she mused, taken with the idea. She hugged Melba around her waist impulsively, slightly startling her. "I'd like that." An impish grin flashed across her face, bringing true loveliness in its vitality and pleasure with life.

"Me, too," Melba said, tucking a strand of hair behind her charge's ear in a maternal gesture. "I'm going to soak up some sun and dry off." She started toward the lounge mattresses lying on the lawn.

At that moment, voices were heard inside the house, coming along the hall toward the library, which opened onto the patio where Melba and Adriane stood. A man and a woman were talking, the woman argumentative, the man amused.

Panicking, Melba whispered, "Where are our towels?"

In the division of labor, Adriane was supposed to supply those while Melba got the mattresses off the lounge chairs and put them on the grass. She had done her part.

Adriane clamped a hand over her mouth. "I forgot them." She glanced around wildly. "Come on, we'll hide until they leave." She ran swiftly across the patio and ducked behind the potted plants next to the house.

Melba had no choice but to follow, slipping behind the miniature fig tree where Adriane had taken refuge. The voices grew louder as the two inside entered the library. Luckily, they didn't come out. Melba kept her fingers crossed that they wouldn't.

The irony of the situation and its amusing side weren't lost on her as she prayed not to be caught hiding in the shrubbery in the nude. It would be too ignoble. What would those people think of her? Why hadn't Hattie warned the swimmers before letting the newcomers into the house?

The angry words of the woman became clear. ''I want to know why you're here.''

An elbow struck Melba in the ribs. She glanced over at Adriane.

''Mother.'' Adriane mouthed the word.

''I happen to live here, remember?'' The laughing male voice was very pleasant to hear in contrast to Glenna Langdon's decidedly angry tones. A shiver raced along Melba's spine at the deep, confident sounds of the masculine baritone.

Two nudges in the ribs. ''Uncle Roth!'' Adriane mouthed, her eyes wide and rounded.

Melba had the distinct impression of being in a falling elevator. Oh, no, she pleaded with Fate, don't let us be seen.

''I will not tolerate any...any *carrying-on* while Adriane is here,'' Glenna stated.

''If you're implying orgies and such, then let me assure you that I don't participate. I prefer privacy.''

His laughter was barely contained. He obviously thought the conversation hilarious.

"Didn't I just see Shirl Bard going into the lounge at Sea Point as I came in the lobby?"

The deep tones cooled slightly. "I've never questioned your eyesight, my dear sister," he said.

"Have you taken up with her again?" Glenna asked, openly daring him to deny what she had obviously concluded.

"Is that really any of your business?" he asked softly.

"It is if you're going to bring her over here and have her sleep over."

"Since when have you taken to censoring my guest list?" Roth Webster was no longer amused with his sister's anger. He found himself impatient with her groundless accusations and implications that he would act in ways that would harm his niece. Hurting Adriane was one thing he would never knowingly do. He moved restlessly across the room toward the open French doors.

Melba worried about the state of her ribs as she received two more nudges from Adriane. "See," the girl hissed, "I told you..."

"Shh." Melba pressed a finger over her lips.

The silence from within the house was becoming unbearably tense. She wished she could see what was happening. She heard footsteps and thought they were near the door. Her heart stopped, then pounded like mad.

Roth blinked, then stared at the images reflected in the panes of the open door. Hiding behind a potted tree were two youngsters: his niece and her friend. A grin spread over his face as he realized their predicament. They had apparently been taking advantage of the isolation of his house to acquire tans all over; now they were trapped outside.

With normal male curiosity, he studied the female figure which hid most of his niece from view. The curve of her leg from thigh to ankle was incredibly attractive. She had small feet with polished, neatly trimmed toenails on her short toes. His gaze wandered over the foliage that screened most of her body, and he watched her bent head wreathed in flowers as she stood perfectly still and stared at the concrete in front of her feet.

Her skin—what he could see of it—was lovely, an even dark gold. Was she that way all over? Water drops sparkled like little jewels on her shoulders from the moisture that still dripped from her tawny gold hair. A sudden breeze stirred the lacy green foliage, and he got a fleeting, tantalizing glimpse of one golden breast. Was the tip the same crushed-strawberry pink as her mouth?

Her entire aura was one of beauty and passion...and innocence. At the same time he felt a contraction of desire invade his loins, he experienced a sadness for what was not to be. At eighteen, nineteen at the most, she would probably consider his age as ancient. But, something in him protested, thirteen or fourteen years weren't too great a difference between them.

My God, what was he thinking! He let his anger with himself build and take over his emotions so that the desire as well as the sadness was dispelled.

Was he so jaded that he had to resort to this woman-child's innocence to restore his zest in life?

No, he answered his own taunting question. No, it wasn't that. But she did seem to represent something he wanted, something that was missing from his life. Like a gift from the gods, she had appeared magically in his garden, a nymph with a garland of snowdrops, and he found he wanted desperately to claim all that was promised just by her being there—life, love, and a continuity with time that stretched into the future through the birth of children.

He looked away from her innocent form, toward the endless blue of the sky, and thought of himself in relation to that responsibility, of holding a wife in his arms, of guiding children on their paths to maturity. Something in him seemed to expand, to grow larger than the space allowed it, and he swallowed hard against the pressure of unexpected emotion. He really was cracking up if the sight of two young girls could do this to him, he decided. He turned back toward the room, determined to protect the privacy of the hidden pair.

Glenna decided to change her tactics. "Roth," she cajoled, "you gave us the use of the house for the rest of the summer, until Adriane goes to college this fall."

"Yes, I did," he readily agreed. "But I don't remember giving up my right to live here, too."

"You know I wouldn't have brought her to this island if I had realized you would be present. A young, impressionable girl like Adriane. She worships the ground you walk on. You have a responsibility—''

''I'm aware of my responsibility to Adriane, Glenna,'' Roth interrupted gently. ''I love the kid. I would never hurt her. But I won't have my life directed by you or anyone else.''

Goosebumps formed all along Melba's arms as his voice rapidly went through several emotional tones while speaking to his sister, going from hard to soft to hard again. He was like quicksilver.

The brother and sister had a lot in common in pure obstinacy, Melba noticed as Glenna spoke up again. ''And I won't have you bringing women over and parading them in and out of your bedroom at all hours.'' Her voice rose in protective maternal warning.

There was another long silence before Roth spoke. His voice was different again, with a deeper tone and throbbing vibrancy in the timbre that hadn't been present when he first entered the library. ''Shirley is visiting with Nigel. He's taken a suite at the resort hotel until the end of next month. I've invited them over to dinner tomorrow night.''

The light tap of high heels could be heard on the terrazzo floor. ''I hope she doesn't get her hooks into poor Nigel,'' Glenna said.

''You certainly have a high opinion of her,'' Roth said with wry amusement. ''I never realized it before now. Why didn't you say something last year?''

''As you say, you won't be given directions,'' she responded in acid-sweet tones. ''I wasn't worried about you. You could handle her caprices, but Nigel is soft-hearted. She might hurt him. Why don't you do something? He's your best friend.''

His soft laughter lightened the air. "Me, save old Nigel from himself? No man appreciates that.'' His voice receded as he crossed the room to Glenna. "Let's go find Hattie, and let her know we're here. She'll want to make something really special for dinner to welcome me home,'' he stated confidently. Laughing again, he ushered his sister out.

Adriane grabbed Melba's arm. "Whew, let's get out of here!''

Melba needed no urging. At a run, they crossed the vacant library, dashed along the hall, and up the three steps into the bedroom wing. Guest rooms opened off each side of the Mexican-tiled corridor. Roth's quarters were at the very end of the wing. He had a suite, Adriane had told Melba, consisting of a sitting area in the large bedroom and a dressing room with twin sinks plus a bath easily big enough for two people. The teenager had giggled upon relating this news.

Behind her closed door, Melba pressed unsteady fingers to her racing heart and waited until she could breathe normally before going into the shower. Under the running water, she discovered the crown of snowdrops as she started to shampoo. She tossed it into the wastebasket.

Chapter Two

Melba quickly washed, rinsed, and dried off. She had to admit that her curiosity to see the intriguing Uncle Roth was causing a tingle of excitement in her as she rushed from the bath to the middle of the bedroom. She stopped abruptly. "Oh, you scared me!" she exclaimed to Adriane who was lying on the bed, dressed in white shorts and a blue top.

The girl tossed the satin harem pillow in the air and caught it expertly, a bright smile highlighting her oval face as she sat up and crossed her legs. "See, I told you they argue all the time now. Things are really starting to happen around here. Let's see, there's Uncle Roth and Mother plus Nigel Stuart and Shirl Bard, all thrown into one pot." A look of glee lit her eyes. "And we'll stir them up good!" she declared.

"Leave me out of the stirring. I nearly had heart failure out there," Melba said, pulling on a pair of comfortable slacks and a yellow knit blouse. Actually, she was delighted with the spirit of mischief Adriane was displaying. It indicated that the girl was well on the road to recovering her equilibrium.

"But wasn't it fun? What did you think of Uncle Roth? Wasn't he simply grand?" Adriane was clearly thrilled with the overheard conversation between her relatives.

"I don't know what I thought," Melba said truthfully, combing her damp hair back and fastening it at her neck with a clip. "I'll have to see him first. One thing I noticed: they both love you."

"I know," the teenager said, suddenly subdued. "I didn't realize how much."

"You deserve it," Melba assured her. "I've discovered you're a very lovable person...when you're not stirring up trouble." She lifted a brow at her young friend.

Adriane laughed delightedly. "Okay, I understand. I'll be good, I promise."

"I'll believe that when I see it." Melba made a face in the mirror at Adriane as she reached for her makeup kit.

"Don't bother," Adriane advised. "There's only family, and Uncle Roth isn't impressed with things like that."

"Let him meet me in all my natural beauty, hmm?" Melba suppressed the thought that he had very nearly done just that.

She was careful not to disparage her own wholesome looks to Adriane; the girl's fragile ego needed building in a positive way that wouldn't be helped by belittling herself. Instead, she acted as if it were an accepted fact that both of them were lovely without artificial enhancement.

"Let's go," Adriane urged, and Melba willingly padded out after her, giving only a fleeting thought to her bare feet. They found the other two in the living room.

Melba stood back while Adriane was kissed and exclaimed over by her mother and uncle. After a few minutes, they remembered her.

"And who have we here?" Roth asked in a throbbingly deep voice as he turned his keen gaze on her. His eyes seemed to take in her entire appearance in a single glance, and she felt that she was being visually devoured.

Grandma, what big eyes you have!
The better to see you, my dear.

As the words of the old nursery story occurred to her, she watched his eyes roam over her figure, then linger on her bare feet as his smile grew.

Superficially, he was similar to her former fiancé in size and coloring, but there the similarities ended. She sensed that the real difference between the two men was one of hardness. This man would let nothing stand in the way of his desires. He would take what he wanted from life and shake his fist in the devil's face while he did. Vitality seemed to radiate from his tall, powerful body.

Frowning, Melba reined in her strange, runaway thoughts. She knew nothing of Roth Webster but the bits Adriane had told her and the muddled impression formed while she was hiding in the bushes.

Scanning his face, she saw features that seemed carved from teakwood. His forehead was broad and smooth, his nose rather prominent but thin. His teeth gleamed with ivory whiteness next to the tan of his cheeks. He was undeniably handsome.

His hazel eyes, liberally sprinkled with green, narrowed on her stormy ones. He sensed her sudden anger and knew it was directed at himself. What had upset her? he wondered. Did she know that he had seen her in a vulnerable moment and resent him for it? No, he was sure she wasn't aware that he had glimpsed her image in the open door.

Her gaze went to his hair, unable to sustain the green fire of his scrutiny. The curling strands weren't blond like his sister's, but were the color of autumn leaves, gold over deep brown. The curls lay in a thick mass about his face, just touching his collar in the back. He took a step toward her, causing her muscles to tighten in recoil.

Adriane, noticing his movement, turned to Melba to introduce her. "This is Melba," she said.

She looks older than eighteen, he thought, staring into her shuttered gaze. She seemed to have an inner poise that allowed her to hide her feelings in the manner of one older and more experienced. "Do you sing?" he asked, wanting to strip the wariness from her and explore her every thought. He had never been so totally captivated by a woman in his life. It was damned scary, he thought.

Thoroughly confused by his question, she could only repeat, "Sing?" She had expected some remark about toast—the usual trite expression—but his question completely threw her.

"Your namesake, Nellie Melba, was a famous Australian opera singer. Have you heard of her?"

She nodded that she had.

"Melba toast was named in her honor; so was peach Melba." He cocked his head to one side. His brows lifted slightly, but there was no arrogance in the gesture. Instead, his face was gently teasing and his eyes gleamed warmly as he watched her confusion spread a glow into her cheeks. "Are you crisp or are you sweet?" he asked.

The strange anger she had felt at his probing stare returned. She sensed that she would have to be on guard around this man. He represented some kind of danger to her, to the newfound peace she had discovered here on his island. She clenched her hands at her sides, willing away the odd thoughts.

"Roth." There was a reprimand in his sister's voice.

"Behave yourself, Uncle Roth. You shouldn't tease Melba. She's suffered a tragic experience." Adriane put her hands on her slim hips and glared at him.

He closed the distance between himself and Melba. Putting a finger under her chin, he lifted his face to study her darkened eyes intently. "What kind of tragedy have you had in your young life?" he inquired softly, speaking only to her.

Adriane answered. "It was a very sad, very tragic love affair, and her heart was broken into tiny pieces. She hasn't gotten over it yet. You're not going to break it again," she ordered in the autocratic manner that seemed to characterize the entire family.

Melba stepped away from his touch. Her face felt hot.

"How can I break it if it's already broken?" he asked in a reasonable tone, while a smile curled the corners of his mouth.

Melba recovered her poise. "My heart is just fine," she stated calmly.

"Good." He sounded satisfied with her response.

"No, it isn't good," Adriane insisted, determined to air the whole tragic episode. "Her fiancé was injured in a car accident two years ago, and then, well, it was a terrible thing and...and Melba was terribly hurt." Adriane floundered as she realized she was breaking a confidence. She clamped her lips firmly together and refused to say more.

"Two years!" Roth exclaimed. His hands shot out and closed on Melba's shoulders. "How old are you?" he demanded.

"T-twenty-five, almost twenty-six," she was startled into admitting.

Roth looked astounded. "Then you're not a friend, a *school* friend, of Adriane's?"

"No." She squirmed in his viselike hold.

Glenna came over. "She's the nurse I told you about. Melba Holly. Really, Roth, what has gotten into you?" Twin lines slanted between the older woman's brows as she frowned at him.

"The nurse," he repeated on a note of wonder which sent vibrant tremors through Melba's blood. His grip lessened, his fingers moving in a caressing way as if reluctant to leave the silken warmth of her skin. "Hello, Melba Holly. I'm very pleased to meet you." His smile beamed on her with heart-stopping brilliance as if he were indeed pleased about something.

He really was a mercurial person, she thought. Points of fire burned in her shoulders, and her anger returned. "How do you do?" she said, forcing a pleasant note into the words. Why did he upset her?

"Fine, thank you," he answered, very solemn, as if replying to a serious inquiry about his health. He smiled again, and Melba was reminded of the breathless way she felt each morning when she greeted the dawn with only herself and the flowers in attendance. She didn't want to feel this way in reference to him.

"I'm going to put on some slacks before dinner," Glenna said. Her hazel eyes, the same shade as her daughter's, scanned the other three with a somewhat worried glance before she left the room.

Without asking, Roth went to a cabinet, selected glasses, and poured a sherry for each of them. He served Adriane first, then brought Melba's glass to her and stayed near, sipping idly at his drink as his gaze roamed her features.

Adriane slipped into a gold and green brocade chair with a happy sigh and started asking Roth questions, catching up with his life and sharing her own since they had last talked. Melba quietly sat on the matching chair, listening and watching as the spirited conversation covered several subjects. Roth, instead of going to the sofa, plopped down on a large brown hassock at their feet.

His green shirt enhanced the verdant flecks in his eyes which were more green than brown, Melba realized. He flicked her with an intense glance that

made her earlier nervousness return. His slow grin
seemed to have an element of mystery to it, as if he
knew a secret but wasn't telling. His eyes went back
to Adriane.

He wasn't at all the way Melba had assumed he
would be. She had been expecting an arrogant,
worldly type of man, but he wasn't. He was definitely self-confident and not inclined to take orders
from others, but there was a gentleness in him, and
an engaging sense of humor that invited a person to
enjoy life with him. The thought was enticing, and
she discovered a longing in herself to do just that.
To laugh freely again, to feel young and full of
life... She dropped her gaze to the glass she clutched
in shaky hands. What had happened to the sense of
rebirth and well-being she had experienced only an
hour or so ago?

She looked up as Roth and Adriane laughed together. His attention and obvious deep affection for
the girl were a positive influence, drawing out of her
a bright, quipping kind of wit that was winsome.
Melba smiled her approval, catching Roth's glance
as she did. He paused in what he was saying to smile
back, then resumed his conversation with his niece.

His attitude toward Adriane indicated he was capable of true, unselfish emotion. Still, Melba reminded herself, a man could love his own family
and be cruel to other women, using them in an un-
caring fashion until he tired of the novelty. Whatever he was, she wanted no part of him. He was
merely her patient's uncle, and she made it a practice not to get involved with other members of a
family. It was against her personal ethics.

"Tell me about this tragic love affair," he invited, turning to her unexpectedly. He noted the determined set of her mouth before she relaxed into an attentive expression that gave away no part of what she had been thinking. He studied her thoughtfully.

Her lips were sensuous in their fullness and enticing with their soft pink shade that reminded him of ripe berries. He wanted to know the taste of her. In his mind, he was having difficulty merging the ever-so-wise nurse he had heard so much about, and whom he had assumed must be a middle-aged matron, with the young, innocent nymph with a crown of flowers he had spied hiding behind the potted fig. The image didn't match his preconceived notions.

The reality of her was even better. She was a mature woman, lovely without being aware of it—a natural seductress with an intriguing wariness and a compelling allure. He drew a deep, careful breath. He wanted to kiss her until she was hot and breathless in his arms, until she lost that cool distance and clutched him, desperate with longing, feverish with desire for him...only for him.

Slow down, he cautioned. She'd been hurt and was as suspicious as a doe that had been previously wounded by a cruel hunter. He sensed he would have to be very gentle with her. It was a new experience for him, to be so perceptive of another. And more than scary—it was terrifying. What had this small silent creature with the stormy-sea eyes done to him?

"You were twenty-three at the time of the accident?" he asked, waiting for her reluctant nod be-

fore he went on. "Did he die in the wreck or later?"
His face reflected his sympathy.

When she didn't answer right away, Adriane supplied the information. "He didn't die, Uncle Roth. Tom was...seriously injured."

His eyes narrowed. Had the man been permanently crippled? Surely she wouldn't have left him because of that. She wasn't the type to desert a person. He probed her eyes and found them closed to him. Absently, he reached out and touched her toe as she crossed one leg over the other. She moved her foot.

Adriane set her empty glass aside and rose. She excused herself and left the room hurriedly as if she were expecting a reprimand for exposing more of Melba's past.

"I should go," Melba said, uncomfortable alone with him.

"Why?"

Forcing her eyes from him, she sought a reason to escape. "To...to put on some shoes before dinner is served," she finally said. She could feel her nerves stretching thinner and thinner, like rubber bands nearing the snapping point.

"You don't need shoes. It's just family, and we're going to eat out on the patio." His eyes swept from her face to her feet, then back, pinning her to the spot. "Were you with your fiancé when he had the wreck?"

His words jarred the newly healed scars of her past. For a moment, she saw Tom's face—his laughing brown eyes, his unruly brown hair—and experienced the despair and remembered the anguish. His family had lived on a farm in Indiana next to her family's farm. Her brother now worked the land there with her father. Tom had been in his last year of medical school when the accident occurred. They had planned to marry as soon as he got out and become a famous husband and wife team, working miracles on their patients.

"No," she said in a strained voice.

He continued his inquisition in spite of the harsh glance he received from her. "His injuries must have been pretty serious."

"I'd prefer not to discuss it, if you don't mind." She couldn't stop her icy rage from spilling over into her words. Who did he think he was, to question her like this? Moving swiftly, she rose and started across the room. "Excuse me, but I think I should change." She clutched at any excuse to leave.

Adriane returned, wearing jeans and a cotton pullover. "You're okay," she assured Melba. She glanced from one to the other, sensing the tension. "What is it?" she asked. "What have you been talking about?"

"I asked her about her fiancé's accident," he explained easily. With deceptively languid movements, he crossed the carpet and stood next to the two women.

"Leave her alone, Uncle Roth. It makes her sad—"

"Not sad," he interrupted, reaching out to grasp Melba's hands, his thumbs forcing her fingers open. "Why are you angry?"

"I'm not." She tried to pull her hands from his. He touched the red semicircles left by her nails on her palms. "I don't like anyone prying into my personal life." She defended herself.

"Or is it that you don't like me?" he asked.

Adriane was amazed at the idea that anyone could dislike her uncle. "She just doesn't know you very well yet." She turned to Melba. "He's concerned. That's why he asked," she explained.

"Thank you for clarifying my motives, little one." He ran a hand through his hair, brushing it off his forehead. His expression, as he turned to Adriane, was warm. "Did I tell you how lovely you're looking? You're growing into a beautiful woman, brat. And making me realize my years." His smile twisted into a wry grimace.

Adriane preened under his compliments. Hooking her hair behind her ears, she studied him thoroughly. "You're not old, but it is time for you to be settling down. Thirty for a man, twenty-five for a woman." She slanted a sly glance at Melba.

Melba groaned inwardly. That was all she needed—a matchmaking teenager for a patient. Roth threw back his head and laughed at the open hint.

"What's so funny?" Glenna asked as she returned to the living room. She had changed into slacks and a long-sleeved blouse.

"Your daughter." Roth contained himself, reaching over to ruffle Adriane's hair affectionately. She grinned unabashedly at him, and he winked at her.

Just as if life were one big joke, Melba fumed, totally confused as to her own emotional state.

"Hattie has dinner ready. Shall we go?" Without waiting for assent, Glenna led the way down the hall, through the library, and out to the table on the patio where the meal was waiting. Five places were set. Melba quickly chose one between Glenna and Adriane. She ignored the quiet chuckle that followed her action. Roth Webster saw too much. He seemed to understand her every move before she even made it. It was unnerving.

When she finished serving, Hattie joined the other four in the casual meal. She and Glenna discussed the menu for the guests who were coming the next night. They decided on a melon cup instead of soup, a light casserole of chicken and garden vegetables for the main course, and pie for dessert.

When they finished, Melba praised the baked fish she was eating. "It has an unusual flavor. I know my landlady in Charleston would love it. Do you give out your recipes?"

Hattie said she would be glad to share it. "The sauce is very easy to make. I'll write it down for you," she promised.

"Thank you." The gray-green eyes sparkled. "I have an ulterior motive in asking for it. I'm not great as a cook myself, but if I give the recipe to Mrs. Wilkins, she'll prepare it and invite me over to dinner.

The conversation veered to food and favorite dishes and the best places to eat. Roth, due to his travels, knew of some place in each major city of the world where the cuisine was outstanding.

"That's one thing that Uncle Roth's wife won't have to worry about," Adriane said smugly.

"What's that, brat?" he asked.

"Cooking. With Hattie around and with you do- ing those flaming dishes you're so good at, why, she won't have to lift a finger.'' She clapped her hands together. ''Aren't we having fresh strawberries tonight, Hattie?''

''Yes, strawberries and cream,'' Hattie affirmed.

''Please, Uncle Roth, flame them for us. It's so pretty.'' She flirted with him, batting her eyelashes outrageously.

''How can I refuse?'' He spread his hands in helpless resignation. ''Come help me get the stuff together.'' The two of them went off to collect the ingredients for the surprise dessert.

''I really shouldn't eat dessert at all,'' Glenna commented, glancing down at her svelte figure in the flattering slacks. ''I'll probably gain ten pounds while we're here.'' She smiled at Hattie in appreciation of the good food the woman served.

''Please don't mention dieting to Adriane,'' Melba requested, at once the professional with her patient's interests at heart. ''She still needs to gain weight, and she's doing so well.''

''Yes, I'll remember, although it is hard to change the habits of a lifetime. It's difficult to think in the opposite vein.'' She touched Melba's arm lightly. ''I want to thank you for coming here. I hope it isn't boring you.''

''No, not at all. In fact, I feel guilty for enjoying myself so much on a job.'' Her pleasure was evident on her face. She stifled the jab of apprehension she also felt.

Glenna smiled the same heart-warming smile that her brother had. ''You're good for Adriane. She likes you, and she trusts your opinion. The doctor said that was important.'' She glanced over her

shoulder to make sure the other two weren't returning. Lowering her voice to confidential levels, she
asked, "Roth does well with her, too, doesn't he?"

"Extremely so," Melba agreed. "He has a very
strong influence on her, and so far, from what I've
seen of their relationship, he's responsive to her
need for male approval."

"Yes," Glenna said slowly. She gazed into the
distance for a second while a sad look crossed her
face. For the first time, lines of age appeared on her
face.

Melba guessed that Glenna was thinking of her
husband and felt pity for the older woman. She reminded herself that the mother wasn't her patient.

In a few minutes, Roth and Adriane appeared on
the darkening patio with a laden tray. With the deft
movements of a magician, he produced a flaming
strawberry concoction which he spooned over
mounds of ice cream in parfait glasses. Adriane, as
his assistant, passed the dessert around the table.
There was a short silence while the treat was sam-
pled.

"Umm, this is delicious. My compliments to the
chef," Melba said, bowing slightly from the waist
and nodding graciously toward Roth. To Adriane
she admitted, "I'm impressed with his ability." That
wasn't all that impressed her about him, she thought,
feeling the stir of sensation inside her that was
caused by his sitting next to her, lightly brushing
her thigh with his as he did.

While Adriane smiled broadly, Roth asked Melba,
"Do you like strawberries?"

"Yes," she admitted. "They're my favorite berry."

His smile gleamed. "I thought so. You reminded me of strawberries the first moment I saw you."

Melba thought his eyes went from her face to her breasts, but in the twilight, she couldn't be sure. A tingling sensation traveled over the hidden skin as if he really were looking at the ripe fullness to be found there.

"What a lovely thought," she said sincerely, refusing to be disconcerted by his penetrating gaze.

"It's getting too cool to stay out. Let's help Hattie get the dishes in," Glenna suggested.

After the task was done, the four left Hattie in the kitchen at her insistence and went into the library. Roth put on some soft music, and they got up a card game, playing with quiet enjoyment until it was time to go to bed.

"If life could always be this pleasant," Glenna murmured later, putting the cards away.

"Then you would be bored," Roth told her. "Life has to be lived as it comes. And it doesn't always come in sugar-coated doses."

Melba glanced up to find his eyes on her while he delivered this philosophic statement. He was probably thinking of Adriane. She replaced her chair in its place next to the desk. While he locked up, the women went to their rooms. Adriane followed Melba into her bedroom.

"So what do you think of Uncle Roth now?" she demanded, sprawling into a yellow boudoir chair, slender legs straight out in front of her.

Melba propped her hands on her hips. "Adriane, are you trying a little matchmaking?"

The teenager looked up with wide, innocent eyes. "Don't you think he would be a super catch?"

"Oh, the absolute limit...for Shirl Bard, maybe."

Adriane straightened up. "Melba! You can't mean that. She's awful. Wait till you meet her tomorrow. Actually," she honestly confessed, "she's not so bad in small amounts, but she's wrong for Uncle Roth."

"So am I. I'm not here to be a summer distraction for him, which is all it would come to, so please don't embarrass me with these not-very-sly hints in front of him. Okay?"

The oval face dropped forward, hidden by the streaky-blond hair. "I'm sorry," she mumbled.

Melba went over and hugged her around the shoulders. "That's all right. I just want things to be clear between us."

The sparkle in Adriane's eyes as she leapt up caused Melba to doubt the sincerity of that apology. "You're a nice person, really nice," Adriane declared. With a brief good night, she went to her own room.

Melba shook her head ruefully and prepared for bed, slipping into her shortie pajamas which made her look all of eighteen. It had been, she thought, one of the hardest evenings in her life. And she didn't think this would be the end of the difficulties, but merely the beginning, if Roth Webster planned to stay around. Darn him, he was as mischievous as his niece...and as appealing, in a strictly masculine sort of way.

His eyes, each time he had held her gaze, had been filled with awareness. The message in those green depths had been unmistakable; he saw her as a woman, wanted her as a man wants a woman. It had been a long time since she let herself see that signal in a man's eyes. With him, she couldn't ignore it.

Her blood seemed to cascade through her veins as, just for a moment, she allowed herself to consider the possibilities. No, she warned herself. She wasn't getting involved in any relationship. She had gone through that once, believing that love could conquer anything in her idealistic youth, but now she knew better. And love wasn't an issue here; it was only chemistry. No, she wanted no part of Roth Webster and the promise in his eyes. She would be on guard.

Chapter Three

Melba examined the skin over her ribs the next morning before she dressed. She didn't have any bruises, which was a surprise considering the pounding she had taken from Adriane while hiding in the bushes the day before.

Laughter shook her slender frame as she considered how it would have looked to Glenna and Roth if she and her companion had been caught in the altogether like a couple of wood nymphs parading about. She would have probably been sent on her way back to Charleston at once. Perhaps that would have been best.

Her mirth faded as she remembered the rest of the day, the meeting with Adriane's much-admired uncle and the cryptic undertones that seemed to penetrate the conversation whenever he spoke to her. Or maybe that was just his technique with women. Her own reactions to him confused her. Something about

Roth Webster made her angry and wary, something else attracted her.

He had such a vast life force, such a vitality to his every movement. There was a sureness about him that spoke of determination to have his way and get what he wanted from life. Was that what she resented—the knowledge that he would not be defeated?

She experienced again the crushing sense of helplessness she had known when Tom had adamantly refused to marry her. Neither tears nor anger had moved him. Because he could no longer give her the life they had planned to share, he had insisted on breaking the engagement. Defeated by his attitude, she had thrown herself into her work until, at last, she had achieved peace within herself. Until Roth Webster had invaded her life, catching her at a moment both embarrassing and vulnerable. Was that why he disturbed her so?

She stared into the mirror as if she could discover some secret in its reflective depths, but she saw only herself. She sensed that her encounter with Roth had left her bruised in some way that didn't show.

The stormy eyes moved thoughtfully down her body as if studying it for visible evidence of injury. Her eyes paused at her breasts whose nipples had darkened in the sun until they resembled ripe berries. What had Roth meant when he said she reminded him of strawberries? That she seemed ripe and ready for plucking?

Her eyes darkened more. She had meant what she had said to Adriane last night. She was no summer distraction for Roth or any man. She had a job to do and that was all she intended to get involved in.

Turning from the mirror, she quickly dressed in shorts and a halter of blue denim. Barefoot, she skipped along to the kitchen for cereal and fruit juice before she went outside to enjoy the first hour or so of the new day alone.

This was the time of day she liked best. It was the interlude of quiet that she needed to restore her own spirit. Adriane slept longer than she did, so, for a while, this island paradise was all hers. Not even Hattie got up before seven o'clock.

This morning the cook was in the kitchen, busy with pots and pans.

"Hello," Melba greeted her cheerfully. "What are you doing up so early? Are you preparing the dinner for tonight already?"

"Heavens, no. Roth will want some breakfast when he comes in," Hattie explained. She mixed batter for pancakes.

Melba helped herself to juice. She was disappointed at the invasion of her private time, but it was his island. He had a right to get up early, too, if he wanted. Glass in hand, she went outside to watch the sun rising over the sand dunes. At least she could have that before he appeared, she thought in growing annoyance.

She went up the steps to the upper patio that adjoined the pool. Birds were chirping a joyous aubade to welcome the day. The air was fresh and cool against her skin. Almost too cool, she noted as a shiver caught her unexpectedly. Breathing deeply, she took a sip of orange juice and almost choked as a tall lean figure rose from the pool, wearing brief, skin-tight trunks.

Roth stood dripping on the pavement a second later. A smile lit his face to devastating handsomeness as he called a "Good morning!" to her. Without haste, he picked up a large towel and began swiping at his brown, sinuous body.

He was gorgeously, flagrantly male. His long, smooth limbs were strongly outlined with muscles that had a look of toughened endurance about them. The dark, curling hairs of his body were slicked straight by the water running down his powerful form.

Melba experienced what could only be described as a gut reaction to his nearly naked presence. Everything in her contracted until only this man dominated her vision and thoughts. A trembling spread throughout her body, a faint quiver of...fear?... longing? It was impossible for her to say.

She was a nurse, she reminded herself. The human anatomy was no mystery to her, male or female. Why hadn't Hattie told her that he was out here, was her next chaotic thought.

His slightly lazy, somewhat lopsided grin widened as he tossed the towel on a chair and reached for a terry robe, slipping it over his arms and broad shoulders, then tying it around his lithe waist.

Melba tore her eyes from his. She knew he had been all too aware of the effect he had had on her. Desperately, she sought an excuse for her stunned response to him. She must be closer to emotional exhaustion than she had realized. For almost six years, she had worked long, hard hours, getting herself established in her career. Then, after the breakup with Tom, she had thrown herself into her job. This was the first real rest she had had in two years.

Roth crossed the patio with long, sure strides. He lifted the glass from her hand, drank over half its contents, and handed it back. "Thanks," he murmured, his voice containing a definite caress.

"You're welcome," she replied, allowing a certain degree of dryness in the tone to show him that she had herself firmly in control now.

He quirked one brow. "Didn't you bring it out for me?"

"Hardly," she said coolly, returning his look. "Had I known you engaged in early morning workouts, I wouldn't have disturbed you." She sipped at the golden liquid to hide her state of nerves, which were now getting shaky at his nearness. She couldn't block out the awareness of his masculine strength hidden beneath the cloth of his robe.

Laughing softly, he said, "You're not disturbing me. At least, not that way. However, bathing beauties who forego swimming suits entirely might, uh, bring out the beast in me."

She stared at him.

"Don't worry. I don't mind. Now about my sister, I can't say. She's turned into some kind of straight-laced guardian of morals the last couple of years."

A tiny gasp escaped her lips, but no further sound would come. Heat burned all over her skin.

"You looked very fetching in your headdress of flowers." His gaze was honestly complimentary. "Delectable," he added, a lingering smile on his face as he took the glass and finished off the orange juice. His eyes skimmed her figure from over the edge of the goblet.

"I'm sorry," she whispered. It was all she could think of to say.

"Don't be," he said quickly. "It was a very pleasant shock to see two naked imps lurking behind the potted plant."

"How did you know we were there?"

"The door was open at an angle. You were reflected in the glass. I would have said something but thought it would be better to get Glenna out of the room so you could make your getaway." His look was gentle.

She turned away. "Thank you." She had never felt so foolish in her entire life.

Hands caught at her shoulders, eased her around to face him. "Hey, it's okay. Don't be embarrassed."

"But I am embarrassed," she cried. "I'm not a kid. I should have known better."

His fingers bit into her skin. "Don't *you* turn into a prude," he ordered, no longer gentle.

She couldn't look at him. Her lashes dropped over her eyes. "You must think I'm a terrible influence on Adriane," she began.

"I think you're a damned wonderful influence on her." He shook her slightly, not hurting her. "You've won her respect and friendship. That's a lot more than most people get."

"Breakfast," Hattie called up to them.

"Come on." He turned them both around, keeping one hand on her arm as if afraid she would flee at the first opportunity. "Let's have something to drink and talk this over. I've been wanting to talk to you since Adriane started singing your praises over a month ago. I'd like to hear your professional opinion on her progress.''

Put like that, she couldn't refuse. After all, that was the reason she was here—to help Adriane and, if necessary, to advise the family on ways they could help the girl.

After making sure they had all they needed, Hattie returned to her room, leaving the two early risers at the kitchen table with large stacks of pancakes to devour along with a rasher of bacon and large glasses of milk.

''By the way,'' Roth said softly when they were alone, ''you have nothing to be embarrassed about. You have one of the most beautiful bodies I've ever seen.''

Again she was at a loss for words.

''Your shyness only adds to the provocation,'' he warned, laughing.

She decided openness was the best policy. ''I'm not that shy. It's that I'm not really used to nude bathing, although I did enjoy the freedom. Mostly, it's something to do with you, the fact that you saw me, I guess.''

The hazel eyes gazed into the candid gray-green ones for a long, soul-searching moment. Then, ''About Adriane. She does seem like a different person even from a couple of months ago. Is this due to you?'' He deftly turned the subject.

''Not really. The staff at the clinic helped her enormously. She understands her reactions to stress now. The two big things in her life recently are you and a young man she met at Sea Point, Greg Aimes." The delicate molding of her lips traced a lovely smile as she forgot herself and spoke of her patient.

"Greg Aimes? I don't know him. How old is he?" Roth asked.

"About twenty. The positive feedback she's getting from both of you is a tremendous boost for her. She's beginning to feel pretty. That alone can make a plain person lovely. And Adriane isn't plain by any means."

He nodded agreement. His eyes roamed the face opposite and seemed to include it in his affirmative opinion.

"That's one of the reasons we've been acting like nature's children around here," she continued her explanation. "I wanted her to accept her body and herself as part of something that was lovely and natural, like the flowers and grounds of this island."

She raised her eyes from her pancakes to watch as his strong teeth bit into a piece of crisp bacon. There was something so intimate about sharing breakfast with a man. It implied a continued intimacy from the night before, she realized.

He handed her a slice of bacon in a gesture that seemed so ordinary that she didn't stop to think about it. She nibbled on it while formulating her thoughts about Adriane.

His deep voice was quietly insistent when he spoke. "I hope you carry on in the same way."

The heat rose in her face again. "It would be okay for Adriane. After all, you're her relative. But I don't think..."

"I'll keep the beast under lock and key," he promised.

She grinned slightly. "I like the idea of equality, but it doesn't really exist. Men are allowed to be exhibitionists, but women are held responsible if they incite men's passions, although I've never been able to see how we can control another's thoughts." A note of resentment crept unawares into her voice. "Or actions."

"I assure you I won't hold you responsible for my lascivious thoughts, and I'll guard my actions...and reactions," he promised, a wicked light gleaming in the hazel eyes. Then he went on seriously, "I think we can work something out. I'll continue my early routine, but I'll guarantee you girls privacy in the mornings, say from about nine until lunch, while I take care of business matters. How does that sound?" His voice, his eyes, invited her to accept the logic of this proposal.

She added more syrup to her half-eaten stack, handing him the pitcher when he indicated he needed more, too. Their fingers touched and a prickling sensation ran up her arm. She was beginning to expect it whenever he was around.

"Fine, but what about your sister?" She licked a drop of sweetness from her lower lip, acutely aware that he watched the movements intently before answering.

"Maybe you can get her to join you. Tell her it's therapy for Adriane. Glenna could use a little relaxing of the schoolmarm ways she's adopted since Adriane started growing up. She certainly wasn't that way when she was younger."

Melba defended her employer. "People have a greater responsibility as parents. They don't want their children to have any bad experiences, so they tend to become overprotective."

"Especially with daughters," he admitted. "I'll probably be the same when I have one." His brilliant smile scorched her heart for a second before he forked a dripping bite of pancake into his mouth.

So he planned to marry and have children someday. She didn't think he would coddle his offspring. He would be loving as he was with Adriane, but he would also expect them to live life to the fullest, taking it as it came, the bad with the good. She was struck by a flashing pain somewhere deep within her; it was as if she were being slowly wrung out, like a sponge being squeezed.

"What is it?" he asked.

"Nothing," she quickly said. Could he see inside her mind as well as he seemed to see beneath her clothing? She would have to be more on guard around him.

He didn't pursue the matter but settled back in his chair after pouring each of them fresh cups of coffee. "So you think I'm doing okay with the kid. My teasing is all right?"

"Oh, yes. She knows you love her. Your joking isn't unkind. Also, when you recognized her as a woman and told her how beautiful she was becoming, it was wonderful for her image of herself. She thinks you're the world's expert on most matters and trusts your judgment completely."

"And you?" he inquired.

"I beg your pardon?"

"You didn't seem to trust my judgment when I told you how beautiful a woman you are."

She shrugged. "I've never been vain about my looks. I'm presentable, even pretty at times, but ordinary."

"Not ordinary," he barked at her with unexpected sharpness. He smiled lazily in the next instant. His eyes seemed to stroke her with tactile glances.

"Really, I'm under no—"

"You remind me of the wild strawberries I used to find in the woods as a child, not large, but luscious and sweet as honey. And sometimes a little tart." He threw back his head and laughed, the way he had last night when his niece had made her remarks concerning their ages.

She tightened her mouth and gave him a look of asperity. He was as incorrigible as the rest of his family.

Pushing back his chair, he rose and stretched, the terry robe in danger of falling open. Smiling, he pulled the ends of the ties to tighten the knot. "I have to go to Sea Point. I'll probably be gone most of the day. Tell Glenna, will you?"

Melba stayed at the table after he had left, sipping the coffee and trying to sort out her feelings, which she found impossible to do. Roth Webster confused her.

She was woman enough and honest enough to admit that he attracted her. His lean, chiseled features and tall, powerful body were exciting and commanding. The delicate curve of her lips moved in an unconscious gesture as if to receive a kiss from firm,

sensuous lips that covered hers in moist, throbbing
fire.

It had been a long time since she had felt the
stirring of passion. She sighed deeply. As a limb that
has had the circulation cut off stings and smarts with
needlelike pain when moved, so her body reacted to
his nearness.

She thought those sensations had been buried two
years ago, but they hadn't. They had merely been
sleeping, dormant like the flowers in the winter cold.
Now she tingled with the stirrings of spring and was
intensely aware of all that season represented in
terms of new life and growth.

The muted roar of the power boat broke into her
musings. Roth had left for Sea Point. She wondered
about the other man, Nigel Stuart. Would Roth do
anything to protect his friend from the model's
clutches as his sister had suggested he should?

Glenna came into the kitchen. "Was that Roth
leaving?"

Melba delivered his message.

Glenna poured a glass of orange juice and a cup
of coffee. She brought both to the table, sitting in
the place Roth had occupied after taking his dishes
to the sink. "Hattie spoils him," she muttered. "All
women spoil him."

Adriane bounced into the room, bringing the very
essence of youth with her. She wore a beach robe.
"Good morning, everybody," she sang out in a me-
lodious voice.

"Would you please tone down that bright cheer?
I just woke up," her mother complained with a
smile teasing the corners of her mouth.

"Yes, Mother dear." The daughter swooped down to plant a kiss on the smooth cheek. "You look so pretty this morning. What have you done differently? Your hair! It's in a ponytail!" She clapped her hand to her forehead. "I can't believe it."

"Oh, get out of here." But Glenna looked pleased at the compliment.

Adriane gulped down a glass of chocolate milk after sticking an English muffin in the toaster. "Who had pancakes?" she demanded, seeing the dishes in the sink.

"Your uncle and I," Melba answered.

"Aha, an early morning assignation," the unquenchable girl stated, obviously delighted with the idea.

Glenna scolded, "Stop it, Adriane. Eat your breakfast. Your jumping around is exhausting me." Turning to Melba, "It's unseasonably hot, isn't it, for the third week in March?"

Adriane butted in. "Maybe you're having hot flashes, Mom. Melba and I go swimming every day after breakfast. You want to join us?"

Glenna hesitated only a second. "I think I will. I'll get my suit." She started to rise.

Adriane grinned and waggled her eyebrows at Melba.

"We just go as we are," Melba said to the older woman. "Hattie keeps an eye out for intruders. Why bother with a suit?"

"You two are young—"

"Oh, come on, Mom," Adriane coaxed.

Melba touched Glenna's arm and nodded an emphatic yes.

"Well, all right, then," she capitulated. The look in her eyes said she was doing this for her daughter.

An hour later, Melba pulled herself up on the edge of the pool and sat with her legs dangling in the warm water. Adriane stood on the end of the diving board, watching her mother perform an excellent backstroke the length of the pool.

The three women could have been sisters. Glenna Langdon was as lovely without clothing as when she was dressed to the hilt. Already Melba could detect a lessening of tension in the other woman. In the tranquillity of this setting, no one could stay uptight. Webster Island was definitely the best place for mother and daughter to become reacquainted without the superficial demands of society.

With a deep sigh of contentment, now that Roth Webster was no longer around to shatter her nerves, she leaned back on her arms and admired the burst of bloom at the end of the grassy area. The azaleas were a solid line of dazzling pink with a white bush or two tucked here and there for contrast. The sky was a flawless blue.

She wondered what the ocean looked like. The dunes hid it from sight on the east, and the house hid the Waterway to the west, so that it seemed they were enclosed in an enchanted valley separate from the rest of the world... Shangri-La at its most beautiful and innocent.

Later, she decided, she would get dressed and climb the stairs over the dunes and walk on the flat beach over there. Down at the southern tip of this island was another island, an uninhabited one. Maybe she could swim across the hundred feet of shallow water between the two and explore the tiny bit of land. That would be fun.

Hattie came up the steps from the kitchen level. "Hot-cross buns," she said, coming to stand at the water's edge.

Adriane greeted the news with a normal teenager's interest in food. "Sounds good!" She dived and swam to the side where the steps were.

"That water sure looks inviting," Hattie said.

"Join us. It feels wonderful." Glenna issued the invitation.

Hattie shook her curly head. "I'd be tempted if I could swim, but I can't," she told them.

"Oh, Hattie, we'll teach you. It's easy. Come on in." Adriane eyed the neat cotton housedress. "Take off your dress and come on."

"No, no." Hattie clucked with quiet, disjointed laughter. "I might try to swim while I was here by myself, and if I drowned, Roth would be aggravated."

They all laughed at this.

"It certainly wouldn't do to inconvenience Roth," his sister remarked, but she was smiling. She walked up the concrete steps built into the shallow end of the pool and slipped into her robe.

"Wasn't that super?" Adriane asked for a general opinion. She wrapped a towel around her sarong-fashion and led the way to the patio table on the lower level.

Glenna sat next to her daughter. "I haven't gone skinny-dipping in a hundred years. It was fun."

Melba guessed that the rest of her family didn't share her restraint. The image of the tall bronze figure of a man climbing from the pool entered her mind.

"Did you use to?" Adriane asked, surprise evident in her face.

"All the time," Hattie answered. "She and Roth were regular water babies. Since she was older, she used to look after him. In fact, she gave him his first swimming lessons before he could even walk and had him swimming before he was a year old."

The young girl looked at her mother with growing admiration. "Did you really?"

Glenna nodded, her face blushing to a becoming pink.

Melba approved the developing closeness between mother and daughter and silently applauded the fact. Adriane was impressed upon learning that her staid mother had actually taught the dashing Uncle Roth when he was a child. Roth had been right about getting Glenna to join them for their morning swim. The naturalness of the environment had led to naturally shared confidences.

After the snack, the three placed lounging mattresses on the grass and relaxed in the sun before going in to dress.

The afternoon passed in lazy good humor. While Adriane worked on the lessons she had to send back to Charleston in order to graduate with her class, Melba wrote her parents and landlady long, amusing letters of her island holiday and the people who were sharing it.

She included an honest description of Roth because her mother worried about her lack of interest in the opposite sex and then worried that her parent might read too much into the letter. Sighing with exasperation, she stuck the pages in an envelope and sealed it before she could change her mind. Roth Webster was beginning to interfere in her every thought!

Going down to the foyer, she laid the letters on the hall table, where they would be taken over to Sea Point by the next person going that way. Quietly opening the front door, she wandered outside, picking a buttercup to twirl between restless fingers. She walked to the pier and stood on its wooden planking, watching the boats plying the Intracoastal Waterway.

The boat she and Adriane used was still tied up in its stall. How had Roth gotten back and forth? Did he phone for someone to come over for him from the hotel?

She was still there when Adriane came swinging down the path, carrying a long, brown envelope and the two white ones containing Melba's letters. "Let's go mail these," the girl called. "Maybe we can find Uncle Roth and give him a ride back."

"Maybe we'll see Greg Aimes while we're scouting around for Uncle Roth," Melba suggested innocently.

Adriane wrinkled her nose at her nurse. "He called for a date tonight, but I put him off until tomorrow. We're going waterskiing. He's bringing a friend for you."

They clambered into the power craft and shoved off. Melba took the wheel. She was familiar with the waters around the islands now and quite good at maneuvering the boat. "How does Roth get to Webster Island?" she asked.

Adriane pushed her flying hair behind her ears. "The hotel rents boats to its customers. He uses whatever is free from those."

Melba nodded her understanding. She expertly pulled into a slot at the marina pier and cut the engine. They hopped out and tied up.

Greg Aimes spotted them at once and came hurrying down the path. "We were just getting up a tennis game. How about a foursome?" he called.

"No shoes," Adriane lamented.

The handsome young man took a girl on each arm and led them to the courtyard. There he introduced them to his friend, Dan, who had arrived for the weekend. The four sat at an outside table and ordered Cokes, talking in a relaxed manner. There wasn't a bashful one in the bunch. That was where Roth found them an hour later.

Melba glanced up to find laughing hazel eyes on her. He looked pointedly at her bare feet, rolling his eyes briefly upward, then shook his head as if giving up on getting her into shoes. She grinned impishly at him.

Roth was enchanted. She moved so easily from girl to woman and back. There was a waiting-to-be-surprised expectancy of youth about her, coupled with a woman's knowledge and experience. For a moment, he considered how it would be to share life with her.

After Adriane made the introductions, he asked

her if they were leaving soon. He wanted a ride back to the island.

"As soon as I mail these." She indicated the letters.

"I'll take them." Melba volunteered to carry them to the front desk where they would be picked up by the postman.

Roth picked up the mail and, taking Melba's arm, escorted her inside. She was terribly self-conscious next to him, aware that they received several interested stares as they went inside, she in shorts, he in dress slacks, wearing a tie with a pastel summer shirt.

At the desk, he noticed the addresses on her letters before he put them in the basket of outgoing mail along with Adriane's envelope. "Your parents live in Indiana?" he asked.

She nodded.

"Mrs. Wilkins—that's your landlady, isn't it?"

"Yes, I live in a duplex; she lives in the other flat. And watches over me like a mother hen," she added, smiling.

He chuckled in his attractive way that made her want to laugh with him. Her skin still burned where he had held her wrist in a loose grip.

"Hello, Roth. I thought you had left," a feminine voice said.

"Just going. We had some mail," he explained, before introducing the two women.

Crossing the lobby a few minutes later, Melba's lips were set in straight lines, and she looked straight ahead.

"What's wrong?" Roth asked, trying not to laugh at her obviously miffed attitude.

"I know it's my fault for coming over here dressed like this, but I wish you wouldn't introduce me to your beautiful female friends when I look like a fright. It's a distinct disadvantage," she complained. "She nearly laughed in my face."

He had no inhibitions about laughing at her. She bore it stoically. "I told you how you look this morning," he reminded her when he could stop chuckling.

The top of her head came to the bottom of his chin. When he put a casual hand on the back of her neck to guide her, she was sure that everyone thought she was his kid sister who had been up to mischief and was being taken home in disgrace.

After saying good-bye to Dan and Greg, they went to the boat. This time Roth was the pilot, and he took them for a short ride in a wide circle around Webster Island and the tiny one adjacent to it.

"Oh, I meant to swim over and explore that island this afternoon," Melba remembered. "Does it have a name?"

"No, not to my knowledge," Roth answered. "It used to be part of Webster." He cast a warning glance at her. "Don't try to swim over. Sometimes there's a dangerous undertow. At certain low tides, you can walk over on a sandbar. I'll watch for it and let you know. Okay?"

"Yes. Thank you."

By the time they docked at their pier, it was time to be getting dressed for the dinner party that evening. Melba wasn't sure she wanted to meet the glamorous model, who had so intrigued Roth last year, but she was curious about the type of female who attracted him. Gorgeous ones, if the one at the hotel was an indication of his tastes.

Adriane burst into her room, wearing a towel and nothing else. "What are you wearing tonight?" she asked.

"I haven't decided." Melba walked over to the closet and surveyed her dresses. "I think this one." She held up a simple summer sheath that Adriane had picked out at her apartment. The smoky green went well with her eyes. "Is it dressy enough?"

"Yes. Could I wear your pantsuit?"

"Sure. Here, try it on." She tossed a flame-colored outfit to Adriane, who caught it easily.

Dropping the towel, the slender girl stepped into the legs and turned so that Melba could zip up the long back zipper when she slipped the material over her body. She waltzed over to the mirror to admire the effect. She looked like a pencil of flame dancing through the muted yellow and white decor of the room.

"It fits, doesn't it?" she asked, an anxious note creeping into her voice.

Melba realized that Adriane dreaded the evening ahead. It was her first social occasion of this nature since she had gotten so ill back in the early winter. "Like it was made for you," she assured Adriane. "I think I'll give it to you. It never looked that good on me."

"You really think it looks nice?" The insecurity behind the saucy facade was touching.

"Very nice," Melba said firmly. "Shirl Bard won't hold a candle to you."

Adriane rolled her eyes. "Wait until you meet her. You're in for a real treat. She drives me batty." With this last exclamation, she dashed out to finish getting ready.

Removing her clothes, Melba went into the bath and filled the tub, adding perfumed oil to the water so that her skin would be silky soft and sweetly scented for the gala evening ahead.

Later, standing in front of the mirror in her underclothes, she applied her makeup with a deft hand, determined not to be thought a schoolgirl when she met the competition. She paused at the thought. Competition?

The familiar throbbing went through her. Don't be ridiculous, she chided herself. She wasn't competing with Shirl Bard for male attention.

With smooth motions, she added deep smoky-green shadow to her eyelids. She selected camellia pink for a blush on her cheeks and a deeper pink for her lips. She wore her hair in a twist at the crown of her head, which she thought made her look more sophisticated.

Adriane returned just as Melba finished fastening her dress and stepped into open-toed sandals. The eighteen-year-old twirled around for Melba's approval.

"You look lovely," Melba said to her young friend. "Let's go put on our femme fatale act."

"Yeah," Adriane agreed with a wry grin. "Or maybe we can dazzle them with our footwork."

Chapter Four

They entered the library arm in arm, both in high heels that added three inches to their stature and with their hair up—Melba's in a twist, Adriane's in a coiled braid—to add maturity. To Roth, the total effect was one of fragile youth and vulnerability in both of them.

Glenna, standing near the door, wore a becoming hostess gown of gold with touches of coral that complemented her blond hair and the light shading of pink on her cheeks she had acquired in the sun that morning.

Melba was almost afraid to look at Roth. When she did, she found his eyes, darkly glowing, on her. A smile lit his face when his gaze reached her feet and the shoes that enclosed them modestly. He passed around the sherry glasses to the ladies, taking something stronger for himself.

As he came nearer and touched her fingers while

handing her the glass, Melba felt as if she had crashed against an invisible shield. There was such vibrant life in him. She turned from it, catching the narrowing of his eyes as she did.

She admitted, with the usual prickling sensation and with a rueful exasperation, that he had to be one of the world's most attractive bachelors. In his dark tan casual suit with an open-throated shirt, he was easily the best-looking man she had ever seen, but he was more than merely physically appealing.

His attractiveness was as involved with his character and personality as with his more obvious attributes. For her, he seemed to symbolize the best of the male persona. The promise of all things good was in his eyes each time he looked at her. Sipping her sherry, she mentally shook her head at these puzzling thoughts while part of her listened to the conversation of the other three.

Outside, the sound of a motor boat dwindled to nothing as it pulled up to the pier. Roth went out to welcome his guests.

Adriane crooked her mouth into a grimace while Glenna patted the neckline of her dress in a nervous gesture that Melba hadn't noticed before. Shirl Bard had an interesting effect on the family. A minute later, the two men and the model came in.

Nigel Stuart was a little taller than average. His oval face and blond hair lent him an air of boyish charm which was enhanced by the easy friendliness of his smile and gray eyes. He wore a white dinner jacket with an azalea bloom tucked into the lapel.

Melba liked the floral accent. She recognized the color from a bush on the path up to the house. His plucking it and sticking it in his buttonhole spoke of humor and impulsiveness.

As her eyes dropped to the woman walking between the two men, Melba's breath caught in her throat. The model was as beautiful in person as in magazine ads.

Her cloud of midnight black hair framed her perfect face. Her dark-blue eyes were expertly made up so that attention was drawn to them again and again. She had a dimple in one cheek.

Her height was no more than an inch taller than Melba's five feet three inches. This, Melba thought, probably explained why she was a photographer's model rather than an haute couture type.

"Glenna! How very nice to see you again." Shirl came forward with her hand outstretched in greeting. Her voice was rather high, like a young girl's, and almost, but not quite, breathless. It was a fascinating quality, and it grated on Melba's nerves the same as if it had been a screech.

"That gown is so becoming. You look like a spring flower," the model continued, swirling a little so that her own midnight blue evening dress fluttered around her sleekness like an enchanted mist.

She released Glenna's hand after the older woman had returned the compliments and made her welcome. Turning to Adriane, Shirl clasped one of the girl's hands between both of hers in an affectionate manner.

"Adriane, you poor child," she commiserated. The perfect lips lifted into a sympathetic smile. "When Roth told me of your illness—"

"I didn't," Roth stated flatly, without expression.

Shirl was undaunted. "Nigel, then." She smiled sweetly over her shoulder at the two men.

An elbow jabbed Melba's ribs. "You're next," Adriane whispered.

"Well," the modulated, breathy voice continued, "when I heard you were under doctor's orders to rest and gain back the weight you had lost, I wished I could change places with you and have to eat to maintain my figure. It's so difficult and tiring to keep to a model's weight."

Melba felt an anger so fierce that a tremor ran down her body in her effort to stifle it. She stared at the floor until she was in control again. One thing she didn't want discussed was the subject of beauty in any context. Adriane was having a difficult enough time coping without being reminded of her own looks, which she thought were inadequate compared to women like Shirl and her mother.

Roth Webster had to share in the blame for his niece's ingrained ideas on attractiveness and desirability. If Shirl were any example—and Melba was sure she probably was—then his choice of female companionship provided poor role models for the young girl.

Setting her expressive lips firmly against each other, Melba decided that she would find a solution to this problem even if it meant taking the wonderful Uncle Roth to task for his thoughtlessness in this regard. She couldn't stand aside while Adriane judged herself by this type of person. Dr. Scott had wanted Melba to head off this very thing.

With another fluttery swirl of her skirts, Shirl

turned to Melba. "And this must be...?" She gave Melba a meltingly sweet smile.

"My nurse," Adriane said dryly.

"Of course. Such a responsibility. I couldn't do it. Sometimes I feel so guilty, just being a butterfly," she explained with a helpless shrug that threatened to cascade the dress down to her waist.

"Butterflies have their uses," Melba observed, returning the smile. "Beauty itself is a reason for being, whether in a painting, a vase"—she gestured toward a sample on a table—"or a person." She was satisfied with the tone in which she had delivered her mini-sermon, relegating beauty to one of many qualities that humans could appreciate in various forms.

"How lovely, how gracious you are." Shirl blinked her great blue eyes rapidly as if emotionally overcome by the compliment. She reached out and touched Melba's hair briefly. "What unusual hair you have. I've known women who have spent a fortune in beauty salons, trying to achieve that kind of brassy shade. Yours is natural, I can tell."

Melba wasn't sure whether to be offended or not. The tone sounded like envy, but the words sounded like an insult. "Yes, it is," she murmured, noting that uncle and niece were having trouble holding their smiles steady.

Adriane clamped a hand over her mouth to keep from laughing as Shirl turned back to Roth, who composed his face in time. Glenna cast Adriane a warning glance to behave herself.

Melba managed to evade the elbow as her patient

leaned toward her to whisper, "I told you she would drive you batty."

For the next thirty minutes, they remained in the library, chatting about the weather and catching up on news of mutual friends.

"Hattie's turn," Adriane announced to Melba.

At that moment, the housekeeper-cook appeared in the doorway. "Dinner," she said to Roth.

"Hattie!" Shirl danced forward, a delighted smile on her face. "I do hope you aren't going to serve anything too irresistible tonight. I gained five pounds on my last visit here." She flashed a sideways glance toward Roth that was secretive and revealing at the same time.

"Shall we go in?" Roth asked. He took his guest's arm and led her to the dining room. Nigel followed with Glenna, and not to be outdone, Adriane grandly held her arm out to Melba, who took it, and they entered behind the others.

In the formal dining room, Roth seated Shirley at his right before moving to the other side of the table and placing Melba on his left. Nigel held the hostess chair for Glenna before sitting on the side next to the model. Adriane sat beside Melba, on her mother's right.

The fruit cups, consisting of cantaloupe and honeydew melon pieces dotted with cherries, were at each place. Shirl admired the Venetian glass of deep green with a gold filigree design around the edge of each compote. The fruit spoon, lying on the matching service plate, was also gold.

"Glenna, this table setting is so attractive." The blue eyes swept over the china and linen. "How refreshingly lovely to use green Venetian glass on white china with green Irish linen under that. And it's so innovative to mix gold and silver flatware,'' she complimented, glancing at the silverware lying on the green tablecloth while holding up the gold spoon.

"That was Adriane's inspiration," Glenna gave credit to her daughter for the color scheme.

"You have excellent taste," Shirl said sincerely, turning her smile on Adriane. "Those arrangements of azaleas are just lovely," indicating the two vases that decorated the table. "The ones in the library with both azaleas and those sprays of forsythia were as well done as any I've seen from a florist."

Adriane pointed to Melba. "Melba did the flowers."

"Oh," Shirl cried softly, "I'm so envious of your talents. You have so many."

"Thank you," Melba replied, forcing as much sincerity into her voice as was in Shirl's.

Under the table, Melba received a nudge on her foot from her neighbor, but she refused to look at Adriane. The girl had been right; Shirl was driving her batty, too. She was just too perfect, too gracious to be real. In recoil, one started looking for flaws in such perfection.

The beautiful model was holding court, manipulating the conversation so that each person got a fair share of attention while she stayed at the very center of all comments. She was quite skillful at it. A person could learn a valuable lesson just from observing the technique.

"Nigel's turn," Adriane whispered.

"Nigel reserved the Azalea Suite at Sea Point. It's my favorite of the penthouse suites." Shirl beamed on the man beside her. "However did you do it?"

Nigel nodded toward Roth, speaking to him as he answered the question. "Bribed the receptionist, of course. I got her to change the reservations. Have you received an irate call from the governor yet?" he joked.

Roth matched his friend's humor. "If I do, I'll refer him to my new assistant—you."

They laughed as Nigel made a dramatic face of dismay.

"Hattie again," Adriane murmured. Glenna gave her daughter a pointed glance. Adriane smiled innocently.

The cook removed the fruit cups and passed around a vegetable salad.

"Hattie, that melon compote was delicious," Shirl said. "What did you use to give it that piquant flavor? It was unusual."

"I marinated it in a liqueur for a few minutes before serving," Hattie answered politely but with no particular inflection.

"I would have never thought of that," Shirl mused with just the right amount of surprise in her voice. "Roth, this woman is a treasure. Don't let her get away."

Did Melba only imagine that the model was suggesting that he had let another treasure slip from his grasp when he had let her go so easily last year?

"He couldn't run me off with a stick," Hattie stated, her shoulders shaking with a silent laugh as she finished her task.

Roth's baritone laughter vibrated on the evening air. "I'd be afraid to take a stick to Hattie. I still remember all the times she used one on me while I was growing up."

Perfectly manicured, shiny pink nails patted his wrist in a mock-scold. "But not near as often as you needed it, I'll bet." The blue eyes opened to their widest, most alluring size.

"Haven't the azaleas been unusually lovely this year?" Glenna took charge of the conversation, changing it from intimate to general tones.

Melba spoke up before Shirl could swallow the bite she had just taken. "Last year, I went to Middleton Place when the azaleas were in bloom. It was like a fairyland. A whole hill of solid pink blossoms under a canopy of trees. I stood on the bridge that crosses the lake and just stared, entranced with it."

Glenna nodded. "I know what you mean. Those are America's oldest landscaped gardens, I think. How long did it take you to tour them? It seemed like we spent ages there."

"Over three hours. I also went into the guest house. Wasn't it terrible that the main house was burned?" Melba was indignant at the thought of the wanton destruction perpetrated by a gang of renegades right after the Civil War.

"Do you like old plantations and ruins?" Roth interrupted.

Her stormy eyes cleared as they flicked to his amused gaze. She reddened at her display of vehemence. "Well, yes, I do. I like to see the clothes and tools used in the past," she began.

"You should have Roth take you to some ruins

over on Hilton Head. It was an old fort, wasn't it?''
Shirl turned to Roth for confirmation.

One dark brow quirked humorously. "As I recall,
it wasn't our most successful date.''

She laughed, exuding charm as she again patted
his wrist. "Let's just say that climbing over old
walls isn't my thing.''

Melba got another kick on the ankle and moved
her feet behind the safety barrier of the chair leg. It
didn't take a lot of imagination to figure out what
the model's thing was—dinner and dances and romantic walks in the moonlight. She didn't need to
look at Adriane's sardonic smile to know that.

With an adroitness that was admirable, Shirl re-
claimed the conversational reins, drawing Roth out
about the resort and his other business enterprises
which she seemed to know well, then turning to
lighter matters to include the other two. Melba was
beginning to get a headache from watching the
smooth performance.

They made it through the salad and into the main
course, which was individual pot pies like her
mother and grandmother made back in Indiana but
with a fancy name. The crust on top was brown and
flaky. Melba and Adriane dug in hungrily. It was
long past the time when they usually ate.

"I really shouldn't eat any of this, but I'm going
to have to sample this heavenly crust. Umm, Hattie
should be ashamed of tormenting me with this delicious food when she knows I have to diet constantly.'' Shirl rolled her eyes expressively.

Adriane hesitated in taking a bite of food. Melba

wanted to choke the reed-slender female across the table.

The breathy voice went on. "It's going to be so delightful when I retire from modeling. I'm going to indulge myself in all my favorite foods." She glanced at the two men from under her long, black lashes. "Perhaps I should get myself a husband before I let myself go, though."

Adriane looked at the delicious chicken pie as if uncertain of its value. She put her fork down without taking a bite and sipped at the small amount of wine that Glenna had permitted her to have with the meal.

Melba searched frantically for some remark that would erase Shirl's implications concerning weight and beauty, but her angry mind could only think of scathing insults which wouldn't do.

"I suppose you are thinking along those lines," Glenna said calmly, buttering a roll generously. "When you get to be over thirty, you start looking positively haggish if you're too thin. Of course when you're young, it doesn't matter so much if you're a trifle slender, but once you're older..."

Smiling compassionately, Glenna looked at Shirl as if she could see the deterioration of those perfect features taking place before her very eyes. Then she bit into the roll.

There followed a beat of nonmovement from the other five, then the two men reached for their wineglasses, Adriane took some time in patting her mouth with her napkin, and Shirl smoothed her hair, using the first nervous gesture that Melba had seen in her.

Following her hostess's example, Melba continued eating, chewing her food with a bland but pleasant expression on her face. Inside, she was choking with glee.

Roth resumed the conversation with that most widely discussed of all subjects—the weather.

"I hope the weather is as nice next month for you as it's been this past month for the girls." He indicated Adriane and Melba while speaking to Nigel and Shirl. "These two have become water babies from what I hear. And according to Hattie, they've convinced my sister to join them."

Glenna smiled. "They'll have her in the water next."

"Not Hattie," Shirl said. "I tried to persuade her last year that she should learn to swim for reasons of safety in case the boat overturned with her, but she wouldn't."

Hattie came in with the dessert. "Humph," she snorted, "it's all I can do to get around on land without floundering around in the water, too." She laughed good-naturedly.

When the plates were taken up, Melba noticed that every casserole dish was empty. Looking up, she saw what could only be a subtle wink from her hostess. Adriane saw it, too. All three of them grinned broadly at each other.

Melba glanced away before she and Adriane could burst into laughter and disgrace themselves. She encountered the hazel eyes at the end of the table. Roth had caught the byplay among the women. He winked in a barely perceptible motion, sharing the private joke with her.

Shirl was back in form. "Cream pie. Hattie spoils

Roth dreadfully. This is your favorite, isn't it, darling?''

Roth arched one brow as he considered. "One of them," he finally conceded. "Lately, though, I find my tastes are changing."

"Must be your age," Adriane jumped into the discussion.

He nodded, his ivory smile flashing across his face. "Probably."

Melba relived that strange, tight sensation as if she were being squeezed inside. He was so handsome when he smiled like that, as if he knew a wonderful secret. She longed to share it with him.

"How are you changing?" Shirl wanted to know, a note of sincere curiosity in her silky voice.

Roth went around the table, pouring a white dessert wine. Hattie checked to see that everyone was served before wheeling the cart with the used plates out to the kitchen. Their host returned to his place, and Glenna picked up her fork when he was seated. They began eating the rich custard pie.

Holding up the clear crystal goblet of wine, Roth studied its contents for a moment. "I think I prefer a lighter touch now. A lighter dessert such as fruit, rather than the heavier creams such as this, although Hattie's custard pie is hard to beat."

Glenna agreed. "I can eat fruit everyday, but pies and cakes are special occasion foods, I think."

"Exactly," Roth said. He sipped his wine appreciatively. "Ah, light and fruity," he remarked, drawing laughter from his guests.

Melba, tasting the pie, wasn't convinced it was only for special occasions. She thought she could eat this delicious concoction daily. Raising her eyes, she was bombarded by Roth's darkly gleaming look as he watched her eat. It made her self-conscious to know he was looking at her.

"Take strawberries," he said casually.

Her hand jerked and she nearly missed her mouth.

Roth glanced at Nigel. "Remember the wild strawberries we used to find in the woods at camp when we played Indians?" he asked. "Firm on the outside with crunchy little seeds, sweet and luscious on the inside. Just the way a woman should be, don't you agree?" he addressed his old friend.

"Absolutely," Nigel held up his glass. "To the ladies," he toasted the women.

"To our charming male companions." Glenna returned the compliment.

Melba hoped her face wasn't ruby-red. She could feel the sheen of moisture forming between her breasts. She thought Roth Webster a blackguard to tease her in front of his family and friends.

"Take the strawberry flower," he continued while she groaned inwardly and promised retribution at the first opportunity. "It's small and delicate, hardly noticeable among the taller plants"—a thoughtful pause—"unless it's invaded a landscaped plant, of course, such as a potted fig.

Adriane choked on her wine. Melba patted her on the back, a grim warning in her eyes as she bent over her young friend. The rest of the group looked interested but a little confused as they waited to hear the point of this story. Roth took a bite of pie.

"How would it invade a potted fig?" Shirl asked, perplexed.

Roth waved his fork negligently. "Well, you know how wild flowers are. They spring up unexpectedly.

Melba could have gladly killed him at that moment. She moved her foot before Adriane could deliver any more significant taps to the two she had already given. If she were able to walk after the meal, she would be surprised. Finally, the dinner was over.

"Shall we take coffee in the library?" Glenna suggested.

There was a scraping of chairs as they stood and filed out of the dining room. Melba wished she could go to her room, but she wouldn't give Roth the satisfaction of knowing he had put her to flight.

The evening wore on, with Shirl resuming her place as center of the conversational wheel, directing the flow of words along the spokes. Each person responded correctly upon receiving a signal and was rewarded by Shirl's smile. At eleven, Roth walked his guests to the pier for the moonlight cruise back to Sea Point.

"What a night," Glenna commented, exhausted. "I'm going to bed." With a wan smile, she left the room.

"Me, too." Melba stood, covering a yawn. Adriane followed her as she went down the hall.

"What did I tell you? Isn't she enough to drive a saint to extremes?" the younger girl demanded, skipping along like a thin flame. She gently nudged her companion in the side. "Uncle Roth saw us," she whispered.

Melba nodded unhappily. "I know."

Adriane giggled. "He didn't mind. And Mother swam with us today. Things are changing." She cocked her head at an angle. "It must be because of you," she continued.

"I didn't do anything," Melba protested.

"You started the nude swimming."

"Yes, and I should have remembered that Eden is full of snakes," she said, forcing a weak grin for her companion.

"I'm going to tell Uncle Roth that you called him a snake." She changed her mind. "No, I won't."

Melba stopped at her door, her smile natural this time. "He probably knows what he is," she quipped. The most attractive wretch I've ever had the misfortune to meet, she said to herself in the privacy of her room a few seconds later. She frowned as she went over the tense evening she had just lived through.

Shirl Bard had to be the most socially accomplished person in the world, she thought. Only Glenna Langdon could rival her, as she had proven when she had elected to reprove the model for her seemingly thoughtless remarks.

Melba slipped into shortie pajamas with an elasticized neck and raglan sleeves. She wondered if Shirl's remarks were really so thoughtless. Or were they a way of calling attention to her own beauty at the expense of others? It was difficult to penetrate the charming facade and discover the truth of the person within. That took time.

After washing her face and brushing her teeth, Melba took down her hair. Brushing the "brassy" locks into soft waves around her shoulders, she had to laugh at the model's descriptive term. It was unique; she had never been called brassy before.

Somehow, Roth had defended her looks with his comments about strawberries. That made her feel strange, confused as everything about him confused and angered her—when he wasn't making her laugh with his subtle humor. Suddenly restive, she pulled her seersucker robe over her pajamas, deciding to go to the kitchen for a glass of milk to help her sleep. She left her room, padding silently on bare feet.

At the door to the library, she impulsively went in, crossed it, and went out onto the patio. The moon was brilliant, reflecting off the restless waters of the pool and silhouetting each item in the garden in silver.

She drifted along the edge, then crossed the grassy square, which was cold with dewfall. Like a shy spirit, she glided among the trees, then up the wooden staircase to the banistered pavilion that crossed the dunes. Climbing up on the broad railing, she hugged the robe around her and watched the frolicking path of silver that transversed the surging ocean and led to the brightness of the moon. Except for the slap-slap of small waves on the beach, all was silent. The peaceful scene should have quietened her nerves, but it didn't. She was as jumpy as a suspicious cat.

She shivered again and thought it was too cool to be out here. And foolish. She would probably be locked out and have to pound on a window to wake someone to let her in. She didn't consider who the someone was that she would wake.

The creak of wood attracted her attention. Roth climbed the steps behind her, then came to the railing where she sat. He hiked a hip onto the banister and, without a word, looked at the ocean, too.

She was immediately overpowered by his presence and resented his intrusion into her privacy. Was there never to be a minute that she could go outside and be alone while he was here? The early morning and late night hours had been her times for solitude. She needed those few moments alone for her own sense of renewal. Sensing his penetrating glance, she turned her face toward him.

"Why don't you want me here?" he asked, his voice deeply serious.

"I do," she started, then, "I mean, I don't care where you are." How did he discern her thoughts so quickly and easily?

"You're seething with resentment at this very minute."

"Seething is too strong a word." She denied the term but not the emotion. "It's just that I find it necessary to be alone sometimes," she explained, and then, perversely, resented that, too.

His hand circled the back of her neck, rubbing the tense muscles there. "You resent my intrusion into your privacy." He stated the case exactly. "Is that it?"

"Y-yes," she spluttered. "I know I have no right—"

"I don't think that's all there is to it," he said, bringing her words to an abrupt halt. "You resent me, personally."

"I—you're wrong," she said quickly.

His challenge was barely audible. "Prove it," he whispered. His eyes gazed into hers relentlessly, refusing to release her.

The squeezing sensation in her chest threatened to cut off her breath. "What do you mean?" She tried to disguise the tremor in her voice with amusement, as if she found this whole conversation too silly for words.

His hand tightened on her neck, and she arched back against the pressure that was steadily bringing her forward. "Like this," he murmured as his head dipped to hers.

At the last minute, she turned her face toward the ocean. "Is your ego bruised because another man was with your former girlfriend?" She tried to sound scornful. "Am I a substitute for Shirl Bard?"

"All cats look gray in the dark?" he mused, laughter evident in his tone. "No, I'd never think of you as anyone but yourself, little cat." His voice dropped to a low, intimate level.

His lips glanced along her cheek, striking little blows of fire with each touch. Heat began a slow, insistent pulsing through her veins like an unseen flow of hot lava.

"Don't," she said stiffly, bending back precariously over the railing. She felt suffocated with a yearning that had been building from the moment she had met him, a longing to have him hold her and touch her.

His arm left her neck and slid down her back, his hand resting in the curve of her waist. He moved from the railing, taking her with him, so that they were standing on the wooden decking, the planks rough beneath her feet.

She couldn't allow this to happen, she thought frantically, summoning anger at his unfair tactics. Somehow, he knew she was attracted to him and, with typical male callousness, wasn't above taking advantage of it.

"Prove it," he whispered again, nuzzling along her neck so that his voice was throbbingly vibrant near her ear. He nibbled beguilingly on the lobe before stroking along her jawline with the tip of his tongue, the cooling effect leaving a burning path in its wake.

Just for a moment, she wanted to give herself to the promise of his arms and turn her face toward his kiss. She spread her hands over his chest, warmth filling her palms and caressing each slender finger as she did. His arms tightened around her, bringing her closer.

"I don't have to prove anything to you," she protested.

"Not to me, to yourself," he said, playing havoc with her senses by kissing along her neck to the hollows of her throat. He unfastened the buttons of her robe.

With a rising panic, she pushed against his chest, but her strength was no match for his. "I don't know what you're talking about," she said.

"Yes, you do," he said with a husky note of passion covering the statement. "I've wanted to touch you since the moment I saw you standing on my patio as if you were a statue, just waiting for my kiss to bring you to life…a gift from the gods for me alone.''

She stared up at him, astounded by his comment. And moved by it, too, she realized. He had sounded so wistful.

"If you don't resent me and you don't dislike me, then prove it. A simple kiss, no more.''

"And…and if I do, that will prove to you that I don't resent you?'' she questioned, stalling for time to quiet her fluttering heart but knowing she was going to do it.

"Maybe. Maybe not.'' He shrugged. "It's according to the kiss.''

"That doesn't make sense,'' she began, then stopped. She no longer strained away from him, and she thought he sensed her acquiescence. She shouldn't be doing this, she reminded herself. It was against her personal code. But if it proved to him that she wasn't disturbed by him, then maybe he would be convinced and leave her alone in the future. Vaguely, she wondered if her own reasoning made any more sense than his did.

Slowly, his mouth descended to hers, and she watched as if in a dream. When his lips closed, warm and moist, over hers, she closed her eyes. For a long minute…and eon…she remained immobile, then the hammering in her chest began to pound louder and louder until her whole body was filled with a rushing feeling like water tumbling down a mountain, faster and faster in its dash to the sea. She clutched at his shirt in desperation.

Her resistance melted entirely as passion ignited inside her with the abrupt force of a volcano. Roth had known it was there; somehow, he had known. That fact scared her as much as the searing rush of her blood. She didn't want to feel this way again. It was much too painful when the passion died, leaving only the ache of bitter ashes in its stead. She pulled away from the kiss. "I don't want this," she told him with trembling bravado.

His large hands molded along her back, sculpting her slender form to his, lifting her to her toes, her weight absorbed by his. "How can we stop it?" he asked with a lover's logic, speaking against her lips.

His mouth left hers, explored the cords of her neck, the sensitive places of her throat. He seemed to know her as if he had a map of her body. He explored further and discovered the stretchy nature of her top. Slipping the material down her arms, he paused to gaze at her breasts in the moonlight. They were silver now; they had been golden in the sun. He couldn't decide which was the most beautiful. He only knew she was the loveliest sight he had ever seen.

His passion was full of a fierce tenderness that was new to him. He wanted to guard his nymph in her Garden of Eden and shield her from all hurt and evil. It was a strangely possessive attitude as well as a protective one.

"You're beautiful," he murmured in passionate cadences as his mouth went with unerring accuracy to the fruitlike buds to nibble gently at the sweetness there. He kissed one, then the other as she arched back, this time to give him access rather than to deny it. She was a thing of wonder and delight in his arms. He couldn't believe he had found her.

When his lips came back to hers, she slid her arms around his lean waist inside his jacket, her breasts pressed to the soft cotton of his shirt. He groaned his satisfaction.

At last, he raised his head, reluctantly removing his lips from hers. He studied her for a long minute, then he simply held her against him while they regained control of their wildly pulsating senses. Far out at sea, they watched the lights of a ship cross the silver path of the moon.

When she was able to speak, she asked, "Did you get your proof?" The laughter that was meant to be insouciant didn't quite come off.

"Why don't you want this?" He returned her question with another.

"I don't want to feel passion. It has no place in my life, especially now while I'm here and have a job to do." Frowning up at him, she decided to be honest and open about her feelings. "I do resent you, or more truthfully, what you can make me feel. You attract me, but it isn't something that I want. Do you see?" she asked for his understanding.

"Has there been anyone in the last two years?" he questioned, again without answering her questions.

Looking away, she shook her head. "No. No one." An equal mixture of sadness and longing seemed to assail her, and she sighed deeply, her chest lifting, then dropping visibly.

"You can't hide yourself from life or bury yourself in your work," he told her gently. He took her arm and guided her down the steps, back toward the dark house. "Did it make you sad when Adriane and I talked about your broken engagement?'' he asked, stopping at the bottom of the stairs. ''Does it still hurt you after all this time?''

''I...not exactly. It's just that something happened recently to...to re-open the wounds.''

''Can you tell me?'' he asked, still being gentle with her. It made her want to weep, his gentleness.

She nodded, but it was a moment before she spoke. ''Tom is practicing medicine in my home town. After the accident, an infection developed in a cut in the groin area. He had a fever...very high...and the infection spread. The antibiotics the doctors tried weren't working. By the time they found one that did, he...he was sterile. We wanted children, had, in fact, planned on having two as soon as possible after we married.''

She turned to Roth, and he gathered her into his arms, trying to comfort her.

Taking a deep breath, she continued, for the first time telling the story to another person besides the barest outline to Adriane. ''Because he couldn't give me the children we wanted, he refused to marry me. He said I was young and would find someone else. A few weeks ago, in February, he married a widow back home who had two children. It seemed unfair. We could have adopted children, just as he is going to adopt hers.''

Her voice quivered to a stop, and Roth held her tighter, his earlier passion turning to pity.

She leaned her head back to gaze at him. ''Nothing I could say would change his mind. It was as if he didn't believe my love was strong enough. That hurt.''

"So you threw yourself into your work, keeping a careful distance from men," he concluded.

"From everyone," she said. "Until Adriane. For some reason, I feel very close to her. We both have had to learn to accept a fate we couldn't change. Her parents' breakup was very hard for her, especially coming at the time it did."

"You've been very good with her. Glenna and I both can see that," Roth told her.

As they started forward again, the grass seemed shockingly cold to her feet as she stepped into it. He correctly interpreted her small gasp and swept her up into his arms. She made no protest but held on to him to make it easier for him to carry her. He put her down at the library door.

"Go to bed," he commanded huskily, turning to lock the door behind them.

She scampered off like a wild creature released from a cage. In her room, lying in the dark, she contemplated the encounter between them that had started off in anger, changed to passion, and ended in tenderness. She felt cleansed of her inner anger now, and that in itself worried her. She mustn't allow herself to succumb to his seemingly genuine sympathy. The next thing she knew, she would be totally seduced by him. Was that what he planned? Was his tender care an act to get beneath her defenses? Don't get involved, she told herself sternly. It was a sure road to heartache as well as a bad business practice.

Chapter Five

"How about dinner and dancing at Sea Point tonight, you two?" Greg asked for the date for him and his friend, Dan.

"I don't think I'll be able to move," Adriane exclaimed, lounging against the padded back of the yacht seat. She pushed the flying, sun-streaked hair behind her ear as she tried to eat an apple. In her red bikini, she looked tanned and healthy. Her ribs cast only slight shadows along her sides, for she had gained five pounds since she been at Webster Island.

The four of them had spent most of the day waterskiing and exploring along the Waterway from Port Royal South, north of Hilton Head Island, down to the channel where the Savannah River emptied into the Atlantic. They had taken lunch and snacks with them, compliments of Hattie and the hotel chef. Now they were lazily replete from sun and a good time in each other's company as Greg guided the rented yacht back to the pier at Webster.

Dan, in a gentlemanly gesture that permitted him to touch Melba, held her hair down with a hand curving over her back where it joined her neck while she polished off her apple. At twenty-one, he was younger in age and experience than she, but they had hit it off well. There was no tingle through her skin at his subtle caress, but there was no revulsion, either. He was a nice guy, and she had enjoyed the day on the water with him.

Greg turned into the cove and angled the boat into position for approaching the pier. He cut the engine to a slower speed.

"Look, there's Uncle Roth," Adriane said.

Roth emerged from the path and came down the pier, ready to grab the lines and tie up the yacht to the wooden posts. He stood with his legs slightly apart and his fists doubled on his hips while he waited for them to come into position. He wore only a pair of very faded cutoffs, the loose threads of the raveled edges mingling with the dark hair of his bronzed skin.

Looking at him, Melba saw several images in her mind—the promise in his eyes as if he would share a wonderful secret with her if she would only listen, his smile that could be gentle or taunting, the way he had touched her with his hands, his mouth and his body...his body rising from the pool, strong and capable and manly...his body touching hers, pressing for the response that he had known she was able to give...his body surging against hers, wanting her, making her totally aware of his desire, and finally, the way he had held her, calming them both and making no demands at all. Her eyes searched over him, seeing all this and more, and he stood still beneath her scrutiny until she glanced away.

"He looks like a pirate," she murmured, hardly noticing that she spoke aloud until Adriane started laughing.

The girl grabbed for her camera. "Stay just like that, Uncle Roth," she called, standing and grabbing two quick candid shots of him.

A few seconds later, the boat was secured.

"Hey, Uncle Roth, Melba says you look like a pirate," Adriane, smiling, informed him.

Roth straightened after securing the line and came to the side of the boat just as Melba was being helped out by Dan. She was grabbed around the waist by powerful hands and hoisted over a bronzed shoulder, the air leaving her lungs with a whoosh of surprise.

"Oh, she did, did she?" he questioned with a wicked note in his voice. "What should we do with these wenches, men?" he joked with the younger men.

"Put me down," Melba demanded, her face going red as the bottom of her bikini stretched downward to an immodest degree. Her three friends were laughing rather than coming to her aid.

Melba pushed herself upward with one hand on his bare back while trying to adjust her suit with the other. She could feel the warmth of his body seeping through to her insides, as if a magic blanket of fire were spreading through her.

Against the front of her thighs, she felt the wiry prickling of his chest hair, which was only more noticeable as she thrashed against him. She stopped moving her legs, but then she became aware of his arm encircling them, one large hand clasping her thigh to hold her in place. She groaned slightly as heat spiraled upward from the caress of his hard palm to settle in the innermost regions of her body.

Another picture invaded her mind, one in which he carried her off to a very private place, a tree-canopied, flower-strewn bower, and did strange and wonderful things to her. Oh, help, she silently cried. In another instant, she was going to explode.

With both hands, she pushed frantically against his back, but that only reminded her of how strong he was and how desirable his body felt to her touch, his skin a smooth, warm surface that was searingly erotic when pressed to hers. Every nerve ending in her own satiny skin was clamoring for more of him. And he probably knew just what she was going through!

Laughter rumbled through his chest, making itself felt to her. "Any suggestions?" He invited Greg and Dan to speak up.

"Look up," Adriane called, getting it all on film.

Roth tossed Melba into the air, caught her in his arms, and hugged her to his bare chest. Instinctively, she placed her arms around his neck. They looked into each other's eyes, and, for a second, there were only the two of them in the entire world.

His mouth opened slightly, and her lips parted, ready for the kiss that never came. With something like regret in the depths of his eyes, he broke the visual contact.

"Smile," Adriane ordered.

Shakily, Melba did, but her eyes were stormy with

mixed emotions as she gazed up at her captor after the snapshot was taken.

Greg laid a hand on Adriane's shoulder. "We were trying to get them to come over to Sea Point for dining and dancing this evening, but I think we tired them out too much today." His look questioned Adriane as he told of his plans to Roth.

"Yes," Melba said quickly. "We've had enough activity for one day." She spoke with authority.

Letting her slide from his arms all the way down his body until she was standing beside him, Roth suggested that the young men come back that evening. "I'm going to grill steaks. You can eat with us, then the girls can have an early night. How's that?" He glanced around the group, getting their consent. "Good. See you later."

After waving Greg and Dan off, the three left on the island started for the house, with Roth tucking a female against each side, his arms around their shoulders.

"Have a good time today?" he asked.

"Yes," Adriane said. She yawned extravagantly. "Umm, I think I'll take a nap after a quick shower. What about you?" She leaned around Roth to ask Melba.

"Definitely," Melba agreed.

Long, sensitive fingers pressed her shoulder in an intimate caress, drawing her eyes upward to his. Some special thought seemed to darken his eyes as Roth looked down on her. The message in those depths wasn't lost on Melba. He would like to join her, in the shower and in bed. She would like that, too. He must have read the answer in her eyes, for he smiled slightly and pulled her closer.

Turning from his gaze, she watched the path in front of them, noting the firm placement of his long, rather narrow feet with each step he took. He had shortened his stride to match theirs. A considerate man, she thought, one who knew his own strength was much greater than the female of the species and who adjusted his behaviour accordingly. She was astonished at the press of sudden tears behind her eyes.

In the house, he released her at her door, closing it quietly behind her. Melba heard him carry on a conversation with Adriane as they proceeded along the hall to her room.

She wondered what they were saying, then scolded herself for her curiosity as she went to run a bath. Adding a generous amount of perfumed oil to soothe her skin after the day in the sun, she removed her bikini and slid into the water, feeling it flow around her body like a healing balm. What would heal her heart if she were foolish enough to let it become entangled with Roth Webster and the passionate promise in his eyes?

She woke with a start, rising to look worriedly at the bedside clock. She wasn't late, thank goodness. For one panicky moment, she thought she had missed some important event, but it was early yet. Plenty of time to dress for the cookout tonight.

Lying back against the pillow, she let her dream come back to her. In it, she had been on a boat. Two islands loomed in front of her. On one, Roth beckoned to her, smiling his beautiful, ivory smile that so entranced her.

On the other island, Tom stood. His face, especially his dark, gentle eyes, was inexpressibly sad. She experienced a rush of tears in her own eyes as she remembered his shaking his head at her as if denying her some favor.

Sighing, she acknowledged the denial from Tom. Her subconscious was telling her that there was no future for her with him; he had closed that door irrevocably with his marriage to the widow. Had she refused to get involved with other men because she had hoped he would change his mind someday?

Male denial wasn't the problem with Roth. She knew only too well that her refusal alone kept them apart. Roth wanted her, and he made sure that she knew it. A slight smile curved her lips. Yes, it was incredibly satisfying to her ego to be desired like that by an attractive, wholly desirable man like him. But she wouldn't give in to that attraction. She mentally crossed her fingers as she had when she was a child, to make it true.

Her smile changed to a frown. Although she had a great deal of affection for Adriane, she wished she hadn't taken this case. It was becoming too difficult for her, even though her patient was doing well. Well, she would just have to grit her teeth and carry it through. She couldn't abandon her young friend until she was past all danger of relapse.

Rolling off the comfortable bed, she pulled on her favorite pair of brown slacks and decided on a long-sleeved blouse with brown, beige, and green stripes running down the material. Buff tennis shoes completed the outfit.

After tying a green scarf under her hair and brightening the tone of her lips with pink lipstick, she went to the back patio next to the kitchen to see if she could help Hattie.

Night was falling and the colored outside lights were on. Roth was busy with the grill at the far end of the area. Hattie was putting a tablecloth on the round table. A card table, folded, rested against the house.

"Hi, may I help?" she called to the woman.

"Sure can. Finish these tables for me, if you don't mind?" Hattie pointed out the items on a tea cart. At Melba's assent, she hurried back into the house.

Melba took plates and silver and put them into place at the large table. She puzzled over the nine settings and counted up the number of people on her fingers. She counted the plates again.

Roth came over and began unfolding the other table.

"Counting Hattie, aren't there seven of us?" she asked him. "Hattie, you, me, Glenna, Adriane, and the two fellows. That's seven," she counted on her fingers again.

"Hattie won't be eating with us," he said. "Nigel is bringing Shirl and Babs over to join us. I thought we may as well have a party. I have to leave tomorrow on business."

"How long will you be gone?" she asked as keen disappointment knifed through her. She bit her lip, but the words had already escaped her.

He answered softly. "About a week. I'll hurry,"

he promised in alluring tones that started the hateful throbbing inside her.

She shrugged indifferently, shaking out a tablecloth to go over the card table when he finished locking the folding legs into place. Resentment flared in her. She felt helpless before his charismatic charm. Setting her face in stern lines, she lectured herself on how she was to react around him. But her body ignored the reprimand, continuing to take note of his every move.

Sighing heavily, she decided on the four younger people at the card table—she and Adriane and their dates—with Glenna and Roth at the larger table with their guests. The prospect of the evening loomed dismally before her.

Babs was the beautiful blonde that she had met the previous day at the hotel. This should be interesting, she thought with a cynical twist of her delicate lips. Glenna will definitely have her hands full, because the blonde wasn't the type to take second place to the glamorous model.

Roth strolled down the patio to check the coals again. She threw him a sharp glance from the corner of her stormy green eyes. Never having been a violent person, she found she wanted to pound him with her fists.

His choice of female companions didn't help his niece's situation at all. The beautiful socialites that he dated weren't good role models for Adriane, who wasn't that type of person. She was a sassy tomboy with many loving, endearing qualities that should be encouraged to develop. Babs and Shirl only served to point out her self-imposed inadequacies.

Chewing on her inner lip, Melba decided to speak to Roth in a stern manner about this problem as soon as possible. He would probably tell her to mind her own business, but where her patient was concerned, any aspect of Adriane's life was her business. Her face took on stubborn lines, and she was startled to find the object of her thoughts at her elbow. He was looking at her feet.

"I like you better without shoes," he murmured. "You're not quite so unapproachable." His fingers raked the rounded curve of her jaw in a teasing caress.

Lifting her face from his touch, she protested. "Please, I'm busy."

"You usually are," he answered sardonically. "And surrounded by people, except in the early morning or late at night."

She was glad of the dim light to hide the heat that rushed to her face. The memory of his lithe body rising from the pool was still vividly with her. So was the memory of his kisses.

"Should I do some flowers?" she asked.

"No," he answered shortly and stalked back to the grill, leaving her staring at his broad back.

Feeling perversely wronged, she decided she would anyway and went inside for two crystal bowls to float azalea blossoms in. They formed a nice contrast to the stoneware dishes, she thought, placing the bowls in the center of each table a few minutes later.

Adriane came out and admired the setup. "Here's someone," she said, catching the faint sound of the motor from the pier. "Come on, we'll act as the welcoming committee."

Melba followed the slender, jeans-clad figure through the house and down the pine-needle path. Two boats were coming in, and they caught the lines and tied them to the pier. Her heart sank when she saw the two women with Nigel. They certainly came from the same mold, just with different coloring.

Shirl was wearing skintight white slacks and a pirate blouse with full sleeves of deep royal blue with white polka dots. A matching scarf, tied gypsy fashion, controlled the midnight cloud of hair. Her stiletto-heeled shoes were held on to her feet by two delicate straps.

Babs also wore white slacks, probably from the same designer's house. Her long-sleeved peasant blouse was striped pink and a pink scarf fluttered around her throat. On her head was a pink tennis hat, the brim turned up jauntily in the back. The long, silky hair was caught up in bunches over each ear and allowed to stream over her shoulders.

Strangely enough, they complemented each other, each enhancing the other's looks. And they were smart enough to realize this fact as they stood side by side on the wooden pier like a pair of preening peacocks.

"Cripes." Adriane muttered the one word that said it all.

"I agree." Melba said. They looked at each other's pant and flat shoes and started laughing.

"Do share the joke," Shirl invited in her charming voice. Her smile was pure graciousness.

"Come on up to the house." Adriane remem-

bered her manners, smiling with a composure that
made Melba proud.

Greg and Dan had been staring at the two beauties. Nigel made the introductions, amusement ram-
pant in his eyes. He gave Melba a wink when he
spoke to her. She flashed a grin at him mischie-
vously.

Greg recovered enough to take Adriane's arm as
she turned toward the house and started up the path.
Nigel took Shirl. Dan quickly offered his arm to
Babs. That left Melba to bring up the rear. And that,
she found, set the tone of the evening.

Although Greg performed admirably, he was still
visibly awed by the two women at the large table.
But mostly Melba was pleased with him, as he definitely preferred Adriane's company.

Dan couldn't tear his eyes from them. This fact
didn't bother her, except as it affected her patient.
Adriane worried about Melba's feelings being hurt
by Dan's inattention. Melba could see the concern
in her eyes and tried to smilingly reassure the girl.

Glancing up, Melba found Roth's gaze on her.
She smiled brilliantly at him, then gave him a saucy
look in return for his more serious one, and was
rewarded by his smile and a knowing lift of his
brows.

On impulse, she picked up her wineglass and
sipped from it, looking over the rim as he had done
to her with the orange juice glass the other morning.
Was it only yesterday?

Roth casually reached for his glass and brought it
to his lips in the same gesture. Their eyes challenged

each other in some undefinable manner until Shirl's touch on his arm broke the contact.

Melba replaced her glass and picked up her fork. Her steak was delicious. So were the potatoes, salad, and new peas that Hattie had prepared. The rolls were homemade ones that used mashed potatoes in the recipe. Shirl would probably choke if she knew that.

Adriane leaned toward her. "You and Uncle Roth were flirting," she accused. She was mildly shocked.

"He's cute," Melba confessed impishly. She arched a wicked brow. When Dan stared at her, she fluttered her lashes at him. Suddenly full of her own power and high spirits, she took charge of their table, drawing the young men into a bantering duel, which immediately involved the four of them in excited conversation.

As the evening progressed, the four around the card table laughed and chatted uproariously, while the five at the big table conversed rather sedately. The two beauties found it difficult to gain the center of attention when there was so much hilarity going on behind them.

Glenna, flicking an indulgent parental eye on the merry four, relaxed and directed the flow of talk at her table with Roth helping out competently. Before they had finished, the younger set went into the library and started dancing to Adriane's favorite records. Later, after coffee on the patio, the other five joined them in there.

While Nigel danced with his hostess, Roth danced

with Babs, Dan grabbed Shirl and Greg stuck loyally to Adriane.

Alone, Melba sat on the hassock and dreamily listened to the music. She was tired and wanted to go to her room and go to bed. In spite of her rallying techniques with the young people, she felt immeasurably older than any of them. And hopelessly gauche compared to the five older adults in the room.

With an illuminating flash, she realized that since she had finished her training and started to work, she had lived most of her life on the periphery of other people's lives, first because she was waiting for Tom to finish medical school, and after that, because there had been nothing else in her life to fill the empty spaces.

She was flooded with a sense of confusion and a swirling tangle of emotions that she hadn't encountered since her adolescent days. It was a painful and unwelcome intrusion into her well-ordered existence.

Another record dropped onto the turntable, and the group behind her changed partners, with Roth taking Shirl and Nigel dancing with Babs. Dan was left with Glenna when Adriane and Greg stayed in each other's arms.

Melba spied the twinkle in Glenna's eyes over the young man's shoulder and exchanged a conspiratorial glance with her. When the tune was over, their hostess declared her intention of retiring to her room. She invited everyone to stay and enjoy themselves for the rest of the evening.

Using this moment for her escape, Melba jumped to her feet.

A hand closed on her arm. "Where are you off to?" a male voice inquired.

She frowned up into the hazel eyes. "I think I'll go to bed. I'm tired."

"Come on, stay. You'll make our numbers uneven again if you leave," he said persuasively. "I'll dance with you, so you won't be a wallflower." His teasing glance swept down her slender figure, but suddenly there was no laughter in his expression. Instead, there was darkness and fire, a passionate intensity.

The music started again, another slow song of haunting love. Melba wished it were something else. Her emotions were skittish enough without impassioned songs adding to the effect.

Roth guided her hands around his neck; he placed his own behind her back, holding her so close she could feel every line of his body against hers. He rested his chin on her head while her cheek nestled naturally against his chest. It was heaven and hell all mixed into one.

As they danced, she quit thinking. There was only the here and now...the pressure of his arms around her, the strength of his hard thighs in intimate contact with her own, the contraction-relaxation of his taut muscles as he moved them around in a slow circle. She knew of his desire, could feel her answer in the quickening of her own body.

"You're sweet," he murmured for her ears only. "God, so sweet." His arms felt like steel around her.

She could hear the solid, heavy pounding of his heart while her own heart echoed the beat, both of them seeming to throb in time to the music. They held each other closer, moving to the same rhythm, as the song rose to its triumphant climax and ended.

For a second, they didn't move, and then, simultaneously, their chests lifted in deep breaths and released. Leaning her head back, she gazed up at him, her eyes confused, his dark and unreadable.

Then he turned to Adriane. "Dance with your old uncle, brat. I'm not going to let one of you beautiful women get away from me tonight," he teased gently.

The night wore slowly on. Melba danced with Dan, with Nigel, then with Greg, with Dan again and finally, a fast number with Roth. He was very good on his feet, improvising with a fast step once in a while to send her into laughter at his clowning. He winked and flirted with her extravagantly.

At midnight, she went into the kitchen to make coffee and bring out the dessert they hadn't eaten earlier. Roth came and pushed the trolley up the incline into the dining room and across to the library. Melba opened and closed doors for him on the way.

As she had expected, the two women declined the cake with remarks on their figures, while the rest of the group had generous portions. Adriane didn't let the other women bother her as she ate all her treat.

A subtle change was taking place in the peaceful atmosphere while they relaxed before calling it a night. Without Glenna's influence as hostess and Melba's induced gaiety to distract attention, Shirl began her interweaving of the conversation into a tight web around herself. Babs was equally determined to claim the limelight.

Each of them soon had the two younger men ministering to her vanity. They were thoroughly charmed by the lovely creatures. Roth and Nigel were amused by the whole show, immune to that type of allure.

Melba seethed as Adriane began to lose her bright wit and retreat into her insecure self. She decided to end the evening as soon as Dan and Greg finished their last bite of cake, which seemed to be taking an extra long time. Roth smiled at her when she made an impatient movement and slightly shook his head.

Glancing at his watch, he took charge. "I have a long day tomorrow," he announced, "so it's time to say good night." He rose to his full height, reaching out a hand to each of the two women to help them to their feet.

The rest of the group stood and began moving toward the door. Roth herded them out expertly and had the two boats cast off before anyone quite realized it. Pulling Adriane and Melba to him, he guided them back up the path. "A very nice party, but I'm glad it's over."

"Me, too," Adriane admitted. "I'm sleepy." She went off to her room as soon as they reached the house.

Roth locked the front door and turned out the porch lights while Melba returned to the library and stacked the dishes on the cart, returning the cart to the kitchen when she finished. There, she began putting the used plates in the dishwasher to save Hattie from facing a sinkful of dirty dishes at breakfast.

Feeling eyes on her, she glanced over to find Roth leaning against the doorjamb, his hands in his pockets, a lazy smile playing about his sensuous mouth. Her delicate lips thinned in vexation.

"What is it?" he asked, correctly reading her expression.

She decided on the truth for Adriane's sake. "You and your girlfriends," she snapped.

"Yes?" He loafed over to lean a hip against the counter where she was working.

She rinsed the crumbs off a plate under running water and placed it in the dishwasher while she collected her thoughts. Several uncomplimentary comments raced through her mind. She discarded those, recalling that she hadn't had this trouble with anger disrupting her logic at other households where she had stayed. That fact only increased her turmoil.

"Adriane has been doing extremely well," she said.

"She certainly has. I appreciate your efforts there."

She cast him a look from the corner of her eye. Was he being sarcastic? No, he looked perfectly serious. Well, maybe not *perfectly,* since there was this gleam in his eyes as he gazed down on her.

"Thank you," she said stonily. "Your friends aren't much help, though." She stacked another plate in the washer and started on the cups.

"You're referring to Shirl and Babs, I take it?"

"Of course I'm referring to them," she burst out. "Who else looks like Venus and Aphrodite come to life and living on Earth?" She dared him to disagree as she pressed her lips firmly against each other.

He chuckled in a subdued tone. "An apt description," he agreed.

"And just as vain and self-centered," she declared.

"Uh-huh, beauty always has a need to call attention to itself, the way beautiful flowers developed their colors to attract bees to their honey so they could be pollinated."

Melba drew a deep, calming breath. She finished the dishes and added detergent before closing the door to the washer. "Do you men have to make such fools of yourselves swarming around them?"

"You women like it," he countered her accusation while his eyes darkened with a sensual look at her. He hooked a hand behind her head to massage the muscles along her neck.

"That's not the point!" she practically yelled at him.

"What is?" His hand slipped around to her chin, his thumb moving back and forth across her bottom lip. He watched her mouth as if fascinated with its trembling response. His head dropped slightly toward hers.

"I..." She couldn't collect her thoughts. Her lips parted as she waited for the kiss, but he made no further move. There, in the library earlier, she had planned her attack on him, but now she could only remember the faintest details. "A-Adriane," she managed to whisper.

"Yes." He searched her eyes as both hands clasped her face and tilted it upward.

She pushed his hands from her and moved several feet away from his disturbing presence. "I want to talk to you seriously." She turned on him with a frown.

He crossed his arms over his chest. "Okay." He waited.

Now that she had his serious attention, she didn't know exactly how to begin with her wild idea. "I have this suggestion..."

His brows rose at that. "Order would be more like it," he murmured, his smile lighting his face.

Her chin jutted into the air. "If you wish to take it that way. It's for Adriane." Nervously, she twisted her hands together as she gathered her courage.

"It's all right, sweetheart, you can tell me what's on your mind. I promise not to get violent." He composed his face into a mask of patience as he nodded permission for her to continue.

She put her hands on her hips and demanded, "Did you ever think about jogging along with a...a cute little pony instead of always running around with those racehorses like Shirl and Babs?"

Expecting a roar of laughter, she was taken completely by surprise by his serious statement. "No, I haven't."

"Well, think about it!"

"I've never thought of women in that particular light," he mused. "Not as racehorses and ponies. Although I get what you mean," he hastened to add.

"Surely there must be someone in your circle of friends who is merely pretty or...or just...wholesome, rather than a raving beauty. How can Adriane believe she's beautiful compared to them, or that you don't consider looks the most important part of a woman's charms if she never sees you with any but those types?'' Melba paused, thinking over her words. Yes, she had covered the major grievances she had with him, those that pertained to her patient; the ones she had for herself, such as his words and actions while they were dancing, she would ignore.

He stroked his chin, lost in thought. Finally, he nodded. ''Yes, you're right, absolutely right.''

She was taken aback by his easy capitulation. ''Well, I'm glad you see that,'' she said, still suspicious of victory.

Roth controlled his elation as one plan after another formed in his mind. All he really wanted to do was grab this bit of womanhood into his arms and kiss the daylights out of her, but of course, he couldn't do that. He had to gain her trust somehow, and that definitely wasn't the way. She knew he wanted her, but desire wasn't enough to win her. He had to convince her there was more. And she had just put the means for doing it in his hands.

''She mustn't be too unattractive,'' he mused as if mulling her advice over. ''But she must be someone with a unique charm of her own and... wholesome, did you say?'' He waited for her nod. ''Yes, wholesome. Fresh. Healthy. Yes, I like the idea. A person who is intelligent, so we can discuss lots of things and not be bored with each other,'' he decided.

Melba was amazed at how well he was taking to the idea. From the gleam in his eyes, he already had someone in mind. That was wonderful, she told herself and tried to mean it.

A strange smile quirked the corners of his mouth

as he stood there, looking at her in a peculiar way. He didn't say anything.

Melba glanced all around the room but could see nothing else that needed doing. "Yes, well, that was all I had to say," she said uncomfortably. Why was he looking at her with that cryptic smile playing about his mouth? "I must admit you took it remarkably well, considering the fact that I was telling you how to run your life."

"You thought I would blow my top at you?"

"Yes." She offered him an apologetic smile. "You told your sister you wouldn't be directed by anyone that first time..." Her voice trailed off.

"Ah, yes." His smile widened, and she wished she hadn't mentioned Friday, when he had seen her and Adriane hiding behind the potted fig tree.

"Who did you have in mind for...for..." She was appalled to hear her runaway tongue ask the question without any conscious direction from her shocked brain.

"The cute little pony?" he supplied generously.

She turned away from his probing stare. "It's none of my business," she stated, excusing him from answering.

"I think it is." His tone was deadly serious as he moved to her, standing behind her. Slowly, insistently, his hands on her arms pivoted her to face him once more. His eyes narrowed on hers with unmistakable meaning as he gazed at her startled face.

"You can't mean...not me?" she gasped.

"Yes, you."

"I wasn't hinting that I wanted to be the one. I'm not in your circle of friends. I never thought..."

"Well, think about it!" he mimicked her earlier words but with amusement in the deep, calm voice.

"No!"

His thumbs brushed back and forth on the smooth cotton of her shirt, sending pulsing beats down the skin of her arms. "Why not?" he inquired with a persuasive undertone.

She tore herself from his grasp. "This is not a joke," she told him sternly, using her voice and stance of whiplash authority which, in the past, had been very effective in dealing with people.

It had no effect whatsoever on him. He simply followed her, taking hold of her again. "I'm not joking. Look, what could be more natural? Adriane respects you. She's already indicated that she would like to match us up." His tone was so reasonable, he almost convinced her. "Hasn't she?" he demanded her agreement.

She shook her head vehemently.

"Sure she has. Those remarks about our ages and about my wife not having to cook. I'm not obtuse and neither are you."

"It's only because she's somewhat dependent on us at this moment for her image of herself. She wants to keep us near her, to maintain the status quo," Melba explained.

"Right, so it should work out fine."

"No, because I'm only going to be here another month. She needs a longer example than that. And someone of her own social group."

Anger rippled over his face, causing a tightening of his grip. "Look who's being the snob," he accused.

"I'm not," she said desperately. "But I'll be gone."

"I admit that will make it more difficult. But not impossible. I'll come up to Charleston to visit you. And you can spent your weekends down here all summer."

"I have other cases to work on."

He frowned at that. "You can't live your life through other people. I think you use your nursing as a shield to insulate yourself from *real* involvement with others."

"How ridiculous," she scoffed.

"Is it?" He began to draw her closer to his chest. He had one month. In that length of time, he would get her to agree to marry him. She would let him into her heart and into her bed, or he would join a monastery, by damn!

She spread her hands over his broad, warm chest, knowing it was useless to try and hold him off if he were determined to embrace her. "Really, Roth," she said in exasperation.

"Prove it," he murmured, his eyes going deep, full a potent charm that had her blood rioting and her breath coming in gasps. His chest moved in concert with hers.

She stared at him resolutely, hating him for what he made her feel and remember. "Kissing you won't prove anything, except it's foolish for me to get trapped in passion with you," she whispered hoarsely.

"Be foolish," he cajoled. The tightening in his loins warned him of his growing need for her. He wished she would melt in his arms the way women always did in sexy novels. Darn, but she was stubborn. And he loved her more and more as he learned more about her. This was the one, the woman who had been made for him. She was his gift from the gods, and he wasn't about to let her get away. He couldn't help but smile. He sounded like a romantic sap.

Pushing her arms straight against him and locking her elbows, she shook her head. "I'm here as a professional. My concern is with my patient only, and sometimes I give advice in that regard. I've done that with you, and that's the end of my involvement."

He wanted to shake her. He dropped his arms so abruptly that she rocked back on her heels before regaining her balance. Putting distance between them, he didn't stop until he reached the door, then he turned to face her, crossing his arms and leaning his weight against the edge again. There was nothing relaxed about his stance. His face was carved in stone. "I'll consider your suggestion. For Adriane's sake." He walked out.

Wrapping her arms around herself as if she were suddenly cold, Melba stood in the middle of the kitchen floor, wondering how her life had gotten into such a mess all at once. Two days ago, she had been content with life, or so she had thought. What had happened in that short span of time?

She glanced toward the door that Roth had gone out. There was the answer—Roth Webster. He was probably one of those men who had to make all women fall for him; after all, women were not the only human creatures who were promiscuous.

Hadn't Glenna and Shirl both stated that he was spoiled?

He did arouse her to passion, she admitted that. She was a normal woman with all the instincts of her species. A frown creased the contours of her brow. Those instincts were painfully alive, she had discovered. And all because of Roth Webster.

She gritted her teeth together in fury. Anger, resentment, frustration—all churned within her slender frame. The door opened, and Roth stood there, taking in her mutinous glare.

"Are you coming to bed tonight?" he demanded, sounding just like an irate husband. "I'm waiting to lock up the house."

Color rushed to her cheeks. She lifted her head and sailed across the room to leave. His touch stopped her headlong rush to escape.

"Wait," he requested in such gentle tones that she would have felt like a boor had she not. He checked the back door and turned out the light. Dropping an arm about her shoulders in easy camaraderie, he led her down the hall, up the steps to the first level, down that hall, and up the next flight of steps to the bedroom level. He opened her bedroom door, tilted her chin up with one finger on the sensitive underside and very slowly kissed her parted lips.

She stared at his closed eyes before closing her own.

"I always get what I aim for," he warned her in a rough whisper a minute later.

"I've never doubted it," she replied. Her face was again stubborn.

"One thing: I can't think of females as animals. Flowers, yes; horses, no." He cocked his head to one side. "Shirl is a hothouse rose; but you...you're something else."

His departing smile was filled with messages that she didn't want to read.

Chapter Six

Melba waited until she heard the sounds of the motorboat departing the next morning before she went to the kitchen. The signs of Roth's breakfast were on the table—the used dishes and scattered pieces of newspaper.

Taking her cup of coffee outside after drinking a glass of juice, she climbed the stairs and perched on the railing, gazing out at the churning ocean. Its mood matched hers.

The incoming tide ran swiftly between Webster and the little island that had once been part of it. She believed what Roth had said about the dangerous undertow there.

Feeling rather forlorn and sorry for herself, she tried not to think that she could have had breakfast with him. It wasn't what she wanted, anyway. No affair with the glamorous uncle of her patient. That's out, she told herself harshly. She went inside and fixed a bowl of cereal.

When Adriane and Glenna came in, they discussed the day and decided on a brief swim after breakfast, then a day of shopping on Hilton Head Island. They would eat the evening meal at Sea Point so that Hattie could have the day to herself unless she wanted to go shopping with them.

She didn't. "I started this new thriller last night, and I think I know who the murderer is. I'll finish it."

The other three were amused at her enthusiasm.

"Hattie is a frustrated detective," Adriane observed.

"Not so," she denied. "I'll get my thrills from the book. I don't want the real thing. All that blood and gore!" She shivered at the thought.

Later, riding across the channel, Melba smiled at the cook's taste in literature, then became thoughtful as she remembered Roth's accusation that she hid behind her career to escape life. Was she, like Hattie, content to get her thrills in other ways than living them? The idea troubled her.

For instance, if it were true, then she couldn't be of much help to her patients. If she didn't face the reality of life, how could she expect them to?

On the other hand, she hadn't thought this to be true before she came here. Was she letting Roth manipulate her so he could seduce her? "I get what I aim for," he had honestly told her. Did he really want her when Shirl and Babs were so obviously available?

With an effort, she pulled out of the doldrums and admired an assortment of lovely clothes at the stores they went to. Most of the outfits were out of her price range, but that didn't stop her enjoyment of the color and cut and fabric of the styles.

Glenna bought a hostess gown of deep lavender that caused her eyes to turn a lovely shade of teal, and Adriane found a pantsuit of vibrant coral pink that looked even better than Melba's flame-colored one had on her. With white coral costume jewelry and white evening sandals, she looked as lovely as any teenager who had graced a magazine or poster.

Glenna treated them to lunch before they went back to Sea Point, where she used her influence as sister to the owner to get them into the beauty shop that afternoon. Finally, at seven, they went in to dinner at the resort's casual dining room. The formal dining room was a suit and tie affair only. Adriane told Melba that they would "do" it one night so she could wear her new clothes.

"You can wear that slinky black silk dress. We'll be perfect foils for one another, like Shirl and Babs were last night," she exclaimed. "We'll come over and have dinner and watch one of the floor shows. They have one at ten and one at twelve."

Melba could have shouted with happiness at Adriane's regained confidence. She dropped her lashes in a sexy look. "We'll knock 'em dead, kid," she promised. "Since I don't have a partner, would you like to be my date?" she asked Glenna.

Laughing, her hostess declined. "I'm sure you'll find a more acceptable escort. Perhaps Dan will be back next weekend. Or Roth."

There was a second of silence.

"I'll come stag and scout out the territory," Melba decided, with a poise she didn't feel.

Adriane looked glum. "We did that, remember. Not a proper man in the bunch."

Melba waggled her brows. "Then we'll just have to find an improper one," she declared firmly.

The week settled into a pattern. The three women swam in the mornings and spent a short time sunbathing before lunch. Hattie had taken to bringing her book out to the patio for a midmorning break. She even pulled her skirt above her knees a little to get a tan on her legs, still firm and shapely from the walking she did.

Adriane, the scamp, teased her unmercifully about joining them in the buff in the pool. She promised to teach the cook to swim like an expert within a week.

Hattie finally conceded that she might try it one day. "But in a suit!" she said unequivocally. This earned her a splash and boos from the others.

The afternoons were occupied with athletic events: boating, waterskiing, or playing tennis or shuffleboard. Greg, Adriane, and Melba became a frequent and familiar threesome on the Waterway and at Sea Point.

With the resort pro or a pickup player, they played doubles on the tennis courts. Dividing up, they formed teams with some of the senior citizens for shuffleboard and staged fiercely competitive tournaments for which the losers had to provide the afternoon tea.

Life settled back into the pleasure of their first weeks there. Melba almost became secure in her island paradise once more. But at the back of her mind was the knowledge that Roth would return. He had said so, and it didn't occur to her to doubt his word.

On Friday night, the two younger women went over to the resort for the seafood buffet, then dancing on the patio with Greg. They met Nigel in the lobby. He was alone.

"Hi, Nigel," Adriane called to him in her friendly way. "What's happening?"

"Not much," he said, coming over to them. His pleasant smile spread over his face and his gray eyes ran over them in an appreciative fashion. "You two are looking lovely tonight," he complimented them. "How about taking pity on a lonely man and having dinner with me?"

For this occasion, Melba and Adriane had consulted and decided to wear summerweight cords—Adriane's of light tan, Melba's of pale green—and Hawaiian print blouses that tied at the waist, leaving a delightful glimpse of bare skin in the center.

"Where's Shirl?" Adriane asked.

"In Charleston for a few days. She has a photography session in some of the gardens for her perfume contract."

"Hmm." She cast a suspicious glance at Melba before smiling at him. "In that case, you're welcome to join us. We're meeting Greg on the inside patio for the buffet and could use a fourth to even our numbers." Tucking a hand in his arm, she motioned for Melba to take the other side and off they went to find Greg.

"Are you staying for the dance?" Nigel asked.

"Uh-huh," Adriane replied, catching sight of her boyfriend and waving to him.

"Then will you allow me to escort you?" he gallantly asked Melba.

"I would be delighted," she said, nodding graciously.

What Adriane lacked in tact, she made up for in honesty, Melba thought, taking her place in the buffet line behind the younger couple. The girl had certainly made it plain to Nigel that she hadn't wanted Shirl along. And the quick glance at Melba had expressed her suspicion that Shirl was in Charleston because Roth was there. Nigel had caught the look, too, but it didn't seem to bother him that his girlfriend might be with another man. Melba grimaced internally. These people had different values in life than those she had been raised to respect, she decided.

Greg pointed them to a table he had saved by placing his sweater on it. For a few minutes after they were seated, there was no conversation. They were too busy eating from plates piled high with fish, lobster tails, blue crab, and shrimp plus hush puppies, fritters, and French fries. Side dishes included cole slaw, tossed salad, baked beans, and corn.

"That was wonderful," Melba exclaimed when she could eat no more.

"If I died this minute from stuffing myself, it would have been worth it," Greg added.

"Ha," Adriane scoffed. "You have a hollow leg. He eats as much as Melba and I together," she confided to Nigel.

Nigel raised one brow, looked the three over, and

announced, "But I like the distribution on you two better than on him."

Still smiling, Melba sipped her iced tea and relaxed. Adriane was looking radiant. Greg was good for her in more ways than one. They gave up their table as soon as they finished eating so others could be seated. Drifting down the courtyard, they found a table near the raised bandstand and listened to the music before joining in the dancing.

Nigel was an amusing, interesting escort, Melba found, and the warmth of his attentive gaze drew from her an answering warmth and friendliness which was her natural way with people. They were dancing to a slow number when, with a motion so smooth she almost missed what was happening, he pulled her closer into his arms. His smile was reassuring when she glanced up, not sure whether to retreat or not.

A vision of Shirl and Roth dancing at some night spot in Charleston leaped into her mind. Her movements became a bit stiff before she mentally forced herself to relax within Nigel's embrace once more. His cheek lightly touched along her temple as he lowered his head to hers. When they returned to the table, Adriane and Greg were there. The two women excused themselves.

In the powder room, Adriane turned an inquiring eye on her friend after they were seated at the long makeup mirror. "Well?" she demanded.

Melba waited until another woman freshened her lipstick and went out before asking, "Well, what?"

"What do you think of Nigel?"

"He's nice."

"Are you falling in love with him?"

Melba laughed merrily. "Really, Adriane, mind your manners." She spread a smooth gloss of pink lipstick over her lips, then examined her face critically in the mirror. Pushing a strand of honey-caramel hair back into the barrette on her neck, she decided that was all she needed to do.

"Seriously, are you? I saw the way you two were dancing. It looked awfully close to me." Adriane persisted with her theory.

"No closer than you and Greg."

"That's different."

"How?" With amused exasperation, Melba watched her patient in the glass as she put on lipstick.

"Well, you're more standoffish than I am. That's one thing. For another, both of you are older. That makes you more"—she frowned, trying to find the right word—"not exactly serious or more intense, but some of each of those. I mean, Greg and I really like each other, but we're not in love. Even if we were, we'd be willing to let things develop slowly because we're young and still have college and things like that ahead of us."

An older woman and her two daughters came in with a gust of noisy chatter. She combed the girls' hair and straightened their dresses and reminded them to be on their best behavior before she herded them out again.

"I'm not in my dotage," Melba said gently as the door closed.

"Oh, I didn't mean that you were." Adriane squeezed Melba's arm before absently combing her hair into waves, flipping the ends under. "But you and Nigel would know quicker if this was what you wanted, wouldn't you?"

"I see what you mean," Melba said, understanding her friend's thinking. "We're more mature and experienced; therefore, we should be able to recognize the real thing when it hits us, right?"

"Right."

The gray-green eyes dropped from their reflections to stare at her hand lying idly on her purse. "It doesn't seem to work that way, though," she confessed. "When it comes to love, we all sort of stumble around in the dark, no matter what our age."

Except she hadn't when she had fallen in love with Tom. She had been so sure of her feelings and his. It was only recently that she had experienced these adolescent uncertainties. She didn't try to delve into the reasons why, not at this moment with those discerning hazel eyes boring into her, ready to pick up the slightest betrayal of emotion.

"Then you do feel something for Nigel?" Adriane asked.

Melba shook her head. "Only friendship."

Adriane sighed deeply. "I had hoped...I want you to stay close. I don't want you to go off on another case and leave us."

"We can still be friends. People don't have to see each other every day to maintain a relationship. You just have to work harder at it. For instance, I have some school chums back home that I see once a year, but we keep in touch. When I go home, we always have a million things to talk about." Her smile conveyed a promise. "It will be easy for us. We both live in Charleston. We can visit and call each other any time."

Adriane wrinkled her nose at herself in the glass. "You're right. And I'm a spoiled brat." Her glance became lighter as she looked at Melba. "It's just as well that you aren't in love with Nigel. I think Uncle Roth has plans for you."

Melba smiled sardonically. "What about Shirl?"

"Do you think he's with her this week? I thought that at first, but not now. Once Uncle Roth is through with a woman, he's through forever. She insulted him by going off to a weekend party while he was out of town on business. He won't forget that."

"Are you ready to go back? The men probably think we've been abducted." Melba didn't think Roth would welcome this discussion of his affairs, and she didn't like talking about him and his women. A frisson ran down her back as she recalled that he had decided to add her to his stable of lady friends, for Adriane's sake.

Not stable, her mind automatically corrected, remembering every word he had spoken to her that last night she had seen him. He thought of women as flowers, not horses.

Adriane wasn't to be distracted. "Last Sunday, I noticed the way he danced with you. So did Shirl and Babs. And a couple of times I've seen him looking at you in a funny way, sort of smiling, when you've been too busy to notice. And you flirted with him over your wineglass. And he flirted back!"

"Yes, but that was just in fun. A joke." Melba shrugged.

"That isn't his usual style. He's very discreet, actually. He's never paraded women through his bedroom as Mother said." She giggled at the idea, then sobering, she clutched her chest. "Maybe he's in love with you!"

"Now you are fantasizing. Snap out of it." Melba stood and opened the door.

Adriane swept through. "Wouldn't it be something if you and Uncle Roth married. I could baby-sit for you."

"Enough," Melba ordered.

"Okay," the undauntable teenager agreed. "But it would be something," she added, refusing to give up the idea.

They danced another hour before Melba suggested it was time to go back to Webster Island. The two men walked them down the marina deck to the boat. With sudden inspiration, Nigel invited Melba to ride with him in his yacht and suggested Greg go with Adriane in the other.

"Then Greg can ride back with me, and we men won't have to worry about your safety," he explained plausibly.

The young couple scurried off before Melba could voice a dissenting opinion. Smiling, she let Nigel help her onto his boat. The others left in front of them, taking an easterly direction.

"It looks as if they're going to take the long way home," Nigel commented, laughing. He headed for the western side of the island, the direct route to the pier.

At Webster, he tied up and helped Melba out, walking with her up the path which was faintly lit by a crescent moon and by colored spotlights which, shining through the shrubbery, cast a fairy glow on the scene. Holding her hand, he whistled the last tune they had danced to until they reached the front door. There, he took her into his arms for the traditional good night kiss.

She raised her lips obligingly. Her heart increased its rate as his lips settled over hers in a pleasant caress. She waited for the familiar throbbing to start in her blood, the sign of reawakened passion. But it didn't happen.

When Nigel lifted his mouth from hers, she smiled at him but with a touch of sadness in the curve of her lips. He seemed to sense her disappointment. He touched his mouth to hers once more, lightly, but again, there was no wild response in her even though she willed it to happen.

"Tomorrow for dinner?" he asked.

"I'm not sure if Glenna or Adriane has anything planned. We're coming over for tennis in the morning, could I tell you then?"

"Sure." He smoothed a strand of hair from her face. "Could you use a partner for tennis?"

"Yes. Would you like to play doubles with us?" she invited.

"I'd rather play singles with you." His voice was wry with overt innuendo. "But doubles will be fine." His hand curved around her neck, and he kissed her again, a brief kiss. "Tomorrow, then," he said, opening the door and making sure she was inside before he went down to the pier to wait for Greg.

In her room, dressed in one of her cotton nightgowns, with her hair lying loose on her shoulders, Melba sat in the dark on her bed and evaluated the evening.

Roth and Nigel must have gone to the same charm school. They had very similar techniques, letting the female set the pace but making her aware of their interest. They had probably compared notes while growing up, telling each other what had worked best with the girls they had dated.

She heard Adriane moving around in her room. The girl had come in a few minutes after Melba, stuck her head in the door to say good night, and gone on to her room. Melba was glad she hadn't wanted a talkfest.

Humor brought a sparkle to the thoughtful eyes as she remembered Adriane's plans to marry her off to Nigel or Roth. How could a person help but love such an irrepressible spirit as that imp possessed!

At last her thoughts returned to the kiss at the door. If her body was leaving its long period of hibernation, why hadn't it responded to Nigel's kiss? And why did she get these wild sensations when Roth touched her? The possible answers to these questions were elusive. Disturbed, she slid under the covers and tried not to think at all.

Roth didn't return to the island the next day or the next. It was Monday before Glenna casually mentioned that he had called and said he was delayed until the weekend.

Shirl was still on her assignment, so Nigel and Melba formed a foursome with Greg and Adriane. They played tennis every day that week. On April Fool's Day, Adriane insisted that they play a game with her tennis balls, which were invisible—according to her.

She called the points, proclaiming the game a tie. They played a sudden-death tiebreaker which she and Greg won when she executed a perfect overhead smash that sent the ball whizzing down the middle of the court—so she said, describing its flight in vivid detail. The gallery applauded her effort.

Each morning the three women swam and sunbathed, acquiring lovely, healthy tans without overdoing it. Each day saw Adriane gain in weight and confidence and grow closer to her mother as Melba purposely brought up topics for discussion in the Garden of Eden setting.

It was a time of contentment, yet Melba sensed that it wasn't real. Things were moving toward a change. What would happen when Roth returned? She dreaded his reappearance as much as she longed for it.

The week passed. On Friday, Nigel took them out in his boat for a long cruise along the Waterway. They had participated in a round-robin tennis tournament that day with only a break for lunch.

The resort chef certainly knew his stuff when it came to food, Melba thought. The luncheon had consisted of cold meats and salads with tiny cakes and fresh strawberries for dessert. The variety had been endless, all of them delicious.

She yawned sleepily, and Nigel glanced from the

water to her for a second. They were sharing the driver's seat. His arm was draped around her shoulders. "Take a nap," he invited, indicating his shoulder.

"I'll wait until we get home," she said, declining.

Although she had been with him every day and night that week, and he had kissed her good night each time he brought her to the house, she continued to keep a definite distance between them. She didn't want to encourage him and then cause him pain if he expected more than casual dating. From the seats behind them, she heard Greg ask Adriane a question.

Adriane called up to them. "Greg just asked about the little island. You wanted to see it, Melba. Would you like to go exploring on it now?"

Roth had promised to let her know when it was safe to cross the sandbar, but he hadn't. She couldn't generate a spark of interest in seeing it at this moment. "I don't think I feel up to it now."

"Me, either," Adriane agreed lazily. "If we're going dining and dancing tonight, I need a nap. Let's go home."

"Aye, aye, captain." Nigel saluted the order smartly. He headed the yacht for Webster Island. Laughing and teasing, the men walked the two women up the path to the door, reminding them that they would see them in three hours.

"And if you want to wear a dress made from the same material as your tennis balls, that's okay with me," Greg informed his date.

"Ho, ho, ho. Very funny," she responded.

Once inside, Adriane told Melba that the men would be knocked off their feet when they saw how gorgeous the two women were going to look that night.

"Are you wearing your new pantsuit?" Melba asked.

"Yes. You wear your black dress. Okay?"

Melba nodded, going into her room. Five minutes later, she was stretched out on her bed, fast asleep. Two hours later, she dashed next door. Adriane was still curled into a ball on her bed.

"Come on, sleepyhead. We only have an hour to make ourselves into those gorgeous creatures you were raving about."

Adriane took one look at the clock, shrieked, and leapt for the bathroom. Melba danced back to her room, humming a nonsensical tune while a gay mood took possession of her. In the bathroom, she hurried through a shower and shampoo, then rubbed some of the bath oil into her wet skin, letting the water rinse it over her body.

After drying her hair, she styled it loose on her shoulders with the ends turned under. Studying it in the mirror, she decided a more sophisticated style was needed for the black dress, which was so elegant in its simplicity. Gathering the tawny locks, she twisted the strands into a coil on top of her head, leaving two spirals to trail down from her temples.

"Now for the face," she murmured, satisfied with her hair. She patted on a liquid base, then outlined her eyes in black, using a mauve shadow and a silver highlighter above that. Using the mascara wand several times, she built her lashes to their thickest and longest. A shiny mauve lipstick added a subtle color to her lips.

She slipped into the black silk, expertly zipping up the long back zipper, then stepped into silver evening shoes. She stuffed a black beaded bag with a small lipstick, handkerchief, and comb, plus some money, which she always carried with her just in case her escort forgot his wallet or she needed to take a taxi home.

Around her throat, she secured a black velvet ribbon with a gold scarab pin. Tiny gold leaves went in her pierced ears.

Adriane came in on a waft of expensive perfume, looking like a dancing flower in her striking outfit of coral. "Are you ready? It's time." Her face was pink with excitement.

Melba spread her arms. "As ready as nature and artifice can make me," she proclaimed. Taking Adriane's arm, she propelled them to the mirror so they could see themselves. Both outfits plunged enough so that the beginning swells of their breasts were visible, enticing the viewer with the promise of concealed delight more than if they had been bare. "Will we do?"

A wide grin spread over the slender oval face. "We'll do," Adriane said emphatically.

The two men arrived, and Glenna saw them off at the door with the admonition to have a good time but be home at a decent hour.

"Not until the witching hour," her daughter called back.

Carefully, Greg and Nigel helped them into the yacht and pushed off. Their escorts were suitably smitten with the beauty of their dates, and Adriane gave Melba a triumphant smile.

Three hours later, replete with lobster, a medley of steamed and artfully seasoned vegetables, and fresh rolls that melted in the mouth, they watched the floor show, which included a comic skit that was outrageously funny without being risqué. Several couples had their children with them and stayed for the show after the meal. Melba thought it was nice for the children to be treated to a glimpse of the grown-up world in this manner.

After the entertainment, the families left, and the dancing began with a small orchestra supplying the music. Nigel stood and reached for Melba.

"Looks like we're just in time," a voice said behind them.

Melba spun around as if on a wild merry-go-round, her mind dizzy as she confronted the smiling couple—Roth and Shirl.

Chapter Seven

"Here's your girl. I'll take mine now. Thanks for looking after her," Roth continued. He guided Shirl toward Nigel and claimed Melba, clamping a strong arm around her waist as he brought her to his side. She stared up into his smiling face.

His eyes glowed with green fire, and he returned her stare for a second before bending to her parted lips. He kissed her quickly, the kiss of a lover who knows he's in a public place but wants to convey the promise of later embraces.

"Shall we dance?" His face changed into its humorous mode with one brow going upward slightly while his mouth wreaked havoc on her senses with its lazy half-smile. She continued to gaze at him without answering. Without waiting for her to collect her thoughts, he gently pushed her in front of him until they reached the hardwood floor, where other couples were already moving in time to the dreamy music.

Taking her arms, he guided them behind his neck as he had that night they danced at his house and, with caressive gestures, placed his own around her slender body until she was firmly clasped against his chest. A sigh rumbled through him as he rested his cheek on top of her head.

"Miss me?" he murmured.

Anger roiled through her. "This is too much," she said through gritted teeth.

"Not enough," he corrected, molding her even closer. His thigh pressed for intimacy against hers.

Leaning her head against his shoulder so that she could whisper directly at him without being overheard by the other couples, she hissed, "How can you be so callous?"

"I just act tough. Inside, I'm a marshmallow."

He was laughing at her. Her fury rose to more dangerous heights. "You...you..." She couldn't think of words sharp enough to pierce his thick hide. "Your arrogance is unbelievable."

"Shh. We'll go outside and talk as soon as the dance is over." He urged her to relax against him in a loving gesture.

Emotion churned within her, but she waited out the intimate dance, not missing a searching look from Adriane as she danced past with Greg. She managed to smile weakly at her patient who was becoming, more and more, a sister to her.

As the music ended, Roth, with a possessive arm around her, led her outside to the garden. He took her to a quiet spot where a bench was partially concealed in an alcove of shrubbery.

"Now," he said.

"You're despicable," she promptly declared. "Just what was that little act all about? The long-lost lover routine." She curled her lip in disgust.

He removed his dinner jacket and slipped it around her shoulders, engulfing her in the warmth generated by his body as if he were holding her. He sat beside her, curving an arm around her so that she couldn't move away, although she tried.

"Be still!" he commanded, for the first time showing impatience with her protesting movements.

She sat rigid as stone and glared up at him.

He chuckled suddenly. "Keep looking at me that way and I'll be forced to kiss you," he warned. "Maybe that's the best idea, anyway. Who needs to talk when we can do more interesting things?"

Melba turned away from his seductive gaze to glare at an innocent bush.

"So what's the problem this time?" he asked, his voice reasonable and amused at the same time.

"You!" She clenched her hands into tight fists, her nails grooving her palms with their imprint, as she reminded herself why she was angry with him. "Just what did you think you were doing in there?"

"I'm just following your suggestion. Remember the cute little pony and all that?" He refreshed her memory.

"And I told you that I don't run in your circles," she snapped. She instantly regretted her temper. This was not the way to handle Roth Webster. Taking herself in hand, she brought her emotions under control. After all, there was no need to make a federal case out of a brief hello kiss and one dance.

His long fingers, infinitely careful, caressed her

arm through the material of his jacket. He watched the turmoil of emotions play through her eyes in the dim light and schooled his rising exultation. The fact that she was disturbed by his presence had to be a good sign, he assured himself. At least, she wasn't indifferent to him, thank heaven.

"I don't run in circles," he chided. "I set a course and head straight for it. Toward you," he added, his voice going to pure velvet. There! He had made his intentions perfectly clear to her.

Desperately, Melba caught his caressing hand to stop its movement. His fingers immediately clasped hers. His free hand caught her other one so that she ended up the trapped one. She changed her verbal tactics, putting ridicule into her tone. "I'm sure Adriane will believe you're interested in me when you've just spent two weeks in Charleston with Shirl Bard."

He lifted his head, taken by surprise at her accusation. "Where the hell did you get a stupid idea like that?" He released her hand and forced her chin up so that she could see the blazing anger in his eyes.

She trembled inwardly at this unexpected wrath. What did he have to be angry about? She was the one made to look the fool. "I should think it's obvious," she said bravely. "You two are gone at the same time for the same length of time and then have the nerve to return together with an air of innocence that would win an award in any movie. If I were Nigel, I'd hit you."

"Nigel happens to be my oldest and closest friend." He ground out the words between his teeth, the muscles standing out like ropes of iron in his jaw. "For your information, I was nowhere near Charleston most of that time. I saw that by working like a demon for two weeks, I could take most of the next three weeks off to be with *you and Adriane*."

She gave a little sniff, indicating her skepticism.

"Listen, I flew to Atlanta where I had a conference with Tor Halliday on a project we're thinking of investing in. I had dinner with him and his very pregnant wife one night. Then I went to New Orleans, met with Reid Beausan to sign the final papers on an office building I'm buying from him, had dinner with him and his moderately pregnant wife— this must be the start of a new baby boom—after which I flew to Nashville about a land deal and back to Atlanta for another conference. I got back to Charleston this morning to find a note from Shirl asking for a ride back here today if I got in on time."

The anger seeped from him as he talked. His voice became richly caressing once more. He thought of how she would look carrying his child, her body curved outward with its weight instead of dipping into the narrow waist that she now had. He slipped his hand inside his jacket to caress along her side, and he felt her stiffen under his touch.

Sighing, he continued, "I called Shirl and told her I'd be leaving as soon as I took care of a few things in town. I did that, picked her up, and came straight here."

"How did you know we'd be here in the formal dining room?"

"I called Glenna before I left Charleston, and she told me you two had already departed for a gala evening with Greg and Nigel. What do you mean dating him all the time I was gone?" he imperiously demanded, his anger rising again at the thought of another man's hands on her as his were. Jealousy was a new emotion for him. Being in love was a lot harder than it was cracked up to be, he thought wryly. Especially this love, which wasn't at all like the feelings he had experienced in college. This was a man's love, not an idealistic boy's. And he knew he must be careful with her.

"I can date whomever I please!"

"Not anymore. You're my girl and don't you forget it." He tapped her on the nose for emphasis, cheerful once more. She wouldn't be so vehement if she weren't as affected by him as he was by her, he reasoned.

She realized it was useless trying to argue with him. He had decided that she was to be the one and that was that, no matter what she thought or wanted. But what were his motives? Was he doing this at her suggestion for Adriane's sake, or had he decided to seduce her, as his actions had indicated on more than one occasion?

"All right," she conceded. "But only for Adriane's sake." She wanted to make that perfectly clear to him.

"Good." He was hugely pleased at her capitulation.

Spoiled male animal, she thought in exasperation. Taking her inside, he folded her into his arms

once more, and she, as part of their act, let herself
be molded to him.

"Enchantress," he breathed near her temple. "I
think you've bewitched me. I love your dress," he
added, running his hands slowly over the silky material along her back.

He was the most aggressively masculine man she
had ever met, full of power and a vibrant force that
seemed indestructible. Yet when he held her, she felt
so safe, protected by his strength from all outside
dangers and from his strength by his own gentle
control. She was helpless against this combination.

Opening her eyes, she encountered the interested
gaze of her friend and patient. Adriane smiled
brightly and significantly at her. Her entire face
glowed with pleasure and approval at the sight of
her uncle and her nurse clasped in each other's arms
in what could only be a passionate embrace.

For the rest of the evening, Melba was rarely out
of those strong arms. Roth claimed her for nearly
every dance, reluctant to share her for even one melody with Greg or Nigel. He didn't dance once with
Shirl, even though she directed several obvious hints
to him that he should.

They left for Webster Island when the second
floor show began. Since the two women had come
over in the yacht, Nigel let Greg have the use of it
to pilot the other three home again.

Roth sat on a padded seat and held a female on
each side of him, keeping them warm and protected
from the wind. He and Adriane talked quietly over
the sounds of the engine.

Melba sat lost in a dream. His attention could go

to a woman's head faster than a fine, rare wine, she realized. She would have to be doubly careful for the next three weeks, now that she had agreed to his boy-meets-girl act.

Curving an arm closer around Melba, Roth passed her door when they returned to the house and escorted Adriane to her room. "Good night, little one, sleep tight."

"I will, Uncle Roth. 'Night, Melba. Don't keep her up too late. We have a tennis game in the morning." With this admonition, the girl entered her room and closed the door, covering a wide yawn as she did.

Roth returned Melba to her door. His head bent to hers.

She averted her face. "There's no need to pretend when she's not around."

"I need the practice." He chuckled. His hand encircled her throat, and with one finger, he touched her jaw to position her head for his kiss. Reluctantly, she met his lips.

His mouth delivered on the earlier promise. He gave her fire and passion, stirring her with a longing to know fulfillment as his tongue parted her lips and tasted the sweetness that was uniquely hers to give. He dipped again and again into the honeyed moistness he found there.

His heart pounded a staccato beat against her outspread fingers as she pushed his coat aside, seeking closer contact with his flesh. He shaped her to him, and her arms went around his waist as she yielded entirely to this magic. While their bodies were held in check, their mouths were given free rein to explore the tempestuous natures that brought them together, each seeking appeasement in the other.

His hands roamed her back, pressing and kneading through the silkiness that separated him from her. He slid the zipper down, easing his hands into the opening he created, being very careful with the fragile material as well as with the woman.

"You're like satin and fire," he murmured. "I want to take you to my room and make love to you all night...forever. I can't touch you enough like this."

His fingers found the small of her back and massaged there, bringing her into the most intimate contact they could sustain, standing there in the dimly lighted hall outside her door. His large hand squeezed her hip as he brought her up hard against him. Easy, he tried to warn his clamoring body, she isn't ready.

Melba heard him make a low, growling sound. It came from deep in his chest, working its way up past his throat as he lavished kisses onto her face and neck, thrilling her with the audible note of his desire.

The scent of her perfume and his after-shave permeated the air around them, increasing the lightness in her head as the mingled aromas rose on the heated wave of their passion. It would be so easy to let herself take this moment and forget all else, she thought through a hazy swirl of emotion.

Guiding the black material down the delicate curve of her arm, Roth freed one breast of the enclosing silk and discovered a small cup of black lace partially concealing the treasure he sought. His eyes blazed over her before his lips descended to nibble at the crescent above the lace. His tongue flicked over the flesh so enticingly hidden.

With a deft movement, he inserted his hand inside the lace while his mouth came back to hers. His skillful play upon her breast carried its own message of his pleasure in her. His mouth swept over her lips in a rush of intense need.

The kiss went on for a long time while her heart pounded and passion ran riot through her slender frame, shaking her into trembling yearning for everything he could give her. He would be a generous lover. She knew that instinctively. And she wanted to bring the same depth of feeling to him, to give him all that she could of a mutual passion.

"Yes," she whispered. "Oh, yes." His lips burned along her throat while his hand continued to caress her.

When he at last lifted his head, his eyes blazed over her upturned face with possessive triumph. The hand that stroked along her cheek in a gentling caress was trembling slightly. "You're an exciting woman," he whispered in a husky voice, rough with longing.

She closed her eyes, unable to meet his gaze. She felt shocked and betrayed by her body. Never had she known such a wild desire. Even though she had acknowledged to him and to herself that he attracted her, she hadn't expected this uncontrollable sense of need to erupt within her. There was a place of savage, primitive passion in her that had never been found before. Why had Roth discovered it while Tom had not?

"Tom..." she began, then stopped at the spasmodic clenching of the arms that held her. She opened her eyes, focusing on his. The narrowed, glittering green of his warned her of his anger, causing her to recoil against his hold.

"It isn't good form to mention one man's name when you're in the arms of another," he said. "Were you pretending that I was your former lover?" He gave her a tiny shake that spoke of violence under strict control.

"No," she denied in a whisper. "I'd never mistake you for Tom."

The fury swept from his face like a wave receding from the beach. His smile bloomed over his dark countenance, casting out the last shadows of his anger. "I'll see that you don't. I'll replace every memory you have of him with a new, fresh, living one of me," he told her, his voice husky with promise. He turned and walked to the end of the hall. At his door, he looked back, his gaze stormily dark, then disappeared inside.

Slowly, Melba went into her room and prepared for bed. It was a long time before her own turbulent thoughts would let her sleep, and when she did, Roth Webster haunted her dreams.

Roth was at the breakfast table the next morning when she entered the room. He wore his ankle-length terry robe, and his hair was damp. Apparently he had already had his morning swim. And his breakfast.

At her entrance, he jumped up, tossed the newspaper aside and held out her chair. Warily, she walked over to it.

"Be seated, madam. I'll have your food in a jif." He put a plate at her place, poured coffee and juice for her, then got hot raisin-bran muffins from the oven and put two on her plate. He added the butter, honey, and a jar of jelly in a semicircle around the perimeter of her place setting. "Anything else for milady?" he asked solicitously.

"I think you've thought of everything," Melba said dryly.

"Oops," he exclaimed. "I nearly forgot." Bending over her, he grabbed a quick kiss. "There. That's everything," he decided, sitting in the chair next to hers and pulling his coffee cup over to him.

He resumed reading the news while she ate, giving her capsule descriptions of items that he thought she would find interesting. When she finished eating, he laid the paper aside.

"How about a kiss of thanks?" he asked when she looked up at him inquiringly.

"No," she promptly stated, stubbornness in every line of her face and posture.

He sighed loudly. "You are the most perverse female, one minute melting in my arms, the next acting as stubborn as a mule—and about as kissable."

With a swift movement, Roth dipped his finger into the butter tub, then rubbed it on her lips.

She was startled. "What are you doing?" she demanded, licking her lips, then wiping them on her napkin.

"Buttering you up, Melba-toast. I think you need

sweetening as well." He dipped his finger in the honey jar. "Here." He sought her lips before the honey could drip.

Melba tried to evade him and maintain a sense of outrage. She could do neither. He was incorrigible...impossible...captivating.

"Turn around here. It's about to drip down your front," he warned. Laughter, barely held in check, rippled through the words, reminding her of the secret murmuring of a mountain brook.

Giving in, she turned her face to his seeking hand and let him smear her mouth with honey. This time, before she could lick it off, his lips were there, doing it for her. He sucked the sweet liquid from her mouth until it was gone.

"You're a menace to society," she told him when he raised his head at last. But she was laughing, too.

"Only to you," he teased, bringing a rapid denial in the shake of her head. He started to lick the remaining honey off his finger.

On impulse, Melba took his hand and guided the finger to her mouth. Using his technique, she slowly and deliberately removed the clinging sweetness from his skin until it was gone and no stickiness lingered. Then she released his hand.

Desire exploded in him, and he thought only of taking her to his room and exploring this wild passion with her for hours without end. He had never wanted a woman so much and in so many ways. If she didn't accept him soon... Patience, he warned himself. His smile was slightly strained. "I know I promised to be responsible for my actions around you, but many more acts like that and I won't be able to keep that promise."

She dropped her head. "I'm sorry," she murmured, embarrassed by the rash action. She didn't know why she had done such a thing.

"No, don't be. I liked it," Roth said softly. "I started it, so I'll just have to take the consequences." He laughed. "Don't worry. I can control my heated passions, for now."

"What's going on in here?" Adriane bounced into the room with her usual morning cheer. Her darting eyes glanced from one to the other as she went to the fridge for the orange juice.

"Nothing now," Roth replied mockingly. He served his niece as he had served Melba earlier, demanding the same tip from her and letting her know that he had already received one such tip that morning.

The teenager gave Melba a nudge under the table.

"Don't break your nurse's leg, brat," Roth ordered, bringing the coffeepot over and warming his and Melba's cups.

Glenna came in a few minutes later. Roth picked up his cup and announced his intention to stay in his study while they did their water ballet.

"We can't swim long," Adriane reminded Melba. "We have tennis at ten with Greg and Nigel. Oh…" She remembered that Shirl was back at the resort.

"I'll take you over. Melba and I are partners," Roth said in no uncertain manner. He walked out with determined strides.

There was a brief silence after his departure while Glenna fixed her plate and joined the other two at the table. Adriane ate one muffin and started on her second, her hazel eyes dark and thoughtful.

At last she spoke. "Uncle Roth was knocked for a loop last night when he saw you in that black dress. He couldn't take his eyes off you all night." She lounged back in her chair, obviously pleased.

"Really, Adriane..." Melba began. She remembered that he was paying court to her, so to speak. And doing a devastating job of it, too, she thought ruefully.

"Don't deny it!" Adriane was not to be put off.

Melba found herself caught in a predicament, unable to dispute the charge as Adriane laughed in triumph.

"What is this?" Glenna asked.

"Uncle Roth and Shirl crashed our dinner date last night. He couldn't keep his eyes or hands off Melba from the moment they arrived." The brown-green eyes danced. "He took her out into the garden for a long time, and he called her Enchantress on the dance floor. I heard him." She giggled as a blush deepened on Melba's face.

Glenna looked worried. "I hope you don't take him too seriously," she started hesitantly.

"Uncle Roth is not fooling around. He's not like that." Adriane defended her favorite relative. "He really likes Melba, and he wouldn't do anything to hurt her or anybody."

Melba patted the girl's arm reassuringly. "Of course, he won't hurt me. We had a lovely chat in the garden and decided we liked each other and that it would be logical for us to form a couple to run around with you and Greg. In fact, Roth has arranged his business schedule in order to do just that. He's going to stay here for the next three weeks.''

"He told you all this?" Glenna asked, looking amazed.

Melba smiled blandly. "Why, yes." It was the truth, although not quite the way she made it sound, as if it had been discussed in utmost friendship.

"Well, well, well," Glenna stated.

"See?" Adriane demanded of her mother, justified in her belief in her beloved uncle.

A few minutes later, they went for a swim, performing their strokes in unison up and down the pool. Hattie brought her book out, hiking her skirt above her knees to get the sun while she read.

At ten, Adriane reminded Roth with a knock on his study door that it was time to go over for the tennis game. He came out, already dressed in his whites.

Melba thought she had never seen such a virile man. Later, when she saw Shirl in her tennis outfit with a blue headband holding her hair back, she thought the same of the model. Shirl was the female counterpart to Roth, she mused.

There was no jealousy in her as she realized this fact. She had never been jealous of another person's looks; beauty was too ephemeral for that. And Roth wasn't interested in Shirl. That was plain to Melba even though Shirl hadn't yet realized it. She felt a sudden sympathy for her. Sometimes beauty could be a hindrance, rather than an asset, in the game of love.

A broad hand settled on the back of her neck,

guiding her onto the court. "Who's going to play us?" Roth called out.

"We are," Adriane shouted, bounding to the far side with Greg right behind her.

Shirl and Nigel went to the next court to play each other. Melba noticed that the model played very well. She seemed to do everything with ease and confidence that were enviable. Nigel won their set, but he had to work for it. They retired to a table while the foursome played out their match.

Roth tempered his game, but he was obviously a bruising player when he chose to be. He and Melba won the match in two straight sets that were respectably close in points.

They joined Nigel and Shirl for lunch in the courtyard patio. Roth seated Melba at his right, taking the position between her and Shirl. Greg was at Melba's right with Adriane sitting between him and Nigel. It was a neat boy-girl, boy-girl, boy-girl arrangement, Melba noted. She was glad Greg wasn't next to Shirl and wondered if Roth had planned it that way.

Everyone ordered the super hamburger platter except for Shirl, who had a salad with no dressing.

The platter consisted of a giant hamburger with all the trimmings plus a special chef's sauce and slathers of sautéed onions spilling out of the poppy seed bun. French fries and slaw accompanied the sandwich.

"Umm, heavenly," Melba murmured, biting into the bun.

Roth leaned toward her in an intimate fashion. "Be sure to eat your onions," he advised.

"I am." Melba smiled with her lips closed because her mouth was full.

He winked across the table at Adriane. "I'll probably want to kiss her later, and since I'm eating my onions, I won't offend her if we both have onion breath." He ended his outrageous explanation and took a big bite of his sandwich.

Shirl looked as if she couldn't believe her ears. Nigel smiled, his eyes going to Melba, while Adriane and Greg laughed out loud.

Shirl laid a perfectly manicured hand on Roth's arm. "You are changing, darling. I don't think I've heard you say anything quite so...well, crude, if you'll forgive me for saying so." Her blue eyes begged forgiveness.

"Feel free to say anything you like," Roth invited. "You're among friends." He wolfed another bite of hamburger hungrily. A slice of tomato started sliding from beneath the bun. He tried to poke it back, but it seemed to have a mind of its own. The entire sandwich threatened to fall apart in his hands. Melba and Adriane giggled at his efforts to hold it together.

"Stop laughing, woman." He glared at Melba.

"You have sauce on your chin," she told him, still giggling.

"Wipe it off," he commanded, still fighting with his meal.

With the long practice of her profession, Melba expertly wiped his chin and mouth with his napkin. After she had finished the task and found several pairs of eyes on her, she comprehended that her ease of manner may have indicated to the others that she had the freedom to touch Roth as she wished; his command made his permission an obvious fact. Troubled, she glanced at Roth who reassured her with his warm smile.

He got his hamburger under control and resumed eating. Shirl began her intricate weaving of conversation, but it became clear from their monosyllabic responses that no one was very much interested in talking.

"What's on for this afternoon?" Roth asked, reclining in his chair with a satisfied air when he was through. His long fingers idly caressed Melba's neck under her ponytail.

Greg spoke up. "A friend of mine lives here and has invited me up to his place. I thought Adriane and I would drop by."

"His parents' house?" Roth questioned.

"Yes. They'll be there, too," Greg hastened to add.

"Fine." Roth's grin widened, a definitely wicked slant to his sensuous mouth. "Now if I could get rid of Glenna and Hattie, I could show Melba my etchings this afternoon." He waggled his brows at her startled, reproving glance. He was unabashedly flirting with her right in front of everyone.

She hoped the heat in her face wasn't too noticeable. If Roth were going to continue for the next three weeks in the manner he had started today, she was going to have to get used to his blatantly sexy remarks or go around in a continuous blush.

Leaning forward in her chair, she ignored Roth and spoke to Greg. "Would you drive my car? It isn't used enough and I'm afraid the battery is going to run down. The office manager has the spare keys. You can use those.''

A little later, she and Roth said good-bye and returned to Webster Island. Shirl had tried to find out what they were doing that evening, but Roth had been noncommittal. He had issued no invitations for anyone to join them.

At the house, Melba went to her room, cleaned up, then wrote long letters to her parents and to Mrs. Wilkins. When she went to the patio, she found Roth and Glenna there, talking quietly about their common affairs, which included several business functions. They asked her indulgence while they settled a few matters between them.

She was flattered that they allowed her to listen to their conversation. Roth stopped a couple of times and explained some point to her so she could follow their line of thought more easily. Glenna didn't seem to mind the interruption.

That night, Greg came over for dinner and all of them, including Hattie, played word games in the library until bedtime. Melba had a marvelous time.

"Happy?" Roth asked, walking down the hall with her while Adriane skipped along in front of them.

"Oh, yes. This evening reminded me of winter nights back home in Indiana. We used to play all kinds of games. Each year, Santa left one gift that was for the entire family, something we could do together.''

"I see."

His voice glided over her senses, deeply vibrant and moving. She was achingly aware of his hand on her neck. She smoothed the material of her sundress nervously, suddenly filled with sensations she didn't want to acknowledge. Being near him made life so difficult for her.

"I'm sure you miss your family, but do you ever feel actually homesick?" he asked at her door.

Adriane waved good night and went along to her room. Melba stared down the hall a moment. "Sometimes, but not since I've been here," she finally said.

He opened her door. "Good night, little one," he said softly before going down the corridor to his quarters. Melba wondered if he realized that he had used one of his pet names for Adriane to her.

That first day of Roth's homecoming was the forecast for the next three weeks. He worked in his study after breakfast each day while the women had their therapeutic swim, then he took them on outings, sometimes shopping on Hilton Head, sometimes just cruising along the waterway.

As a couple, he and Melba played tennis and shuffleboard with other couples, usually Greg and Adriane. Occasionally, Hattie and Glenna came along with them at his insistence for a gala evening, especially when they went over to Sea Point on Friday night for the buffet.

Melba was his date in the eyes of everyone by the end of the second week. They were constantly together. At first, it had been hard for her, but his attitude was so casual that she soon relaxed.

He was a charming, entertaining companion with wide interests. He discussed any topic that came to his mind with her, and she found it was increasingly easy to share all her thoughts with him. He didn't kiss her or push his advantage when they were alone as she had thought he would. He was a perfect gentleman and host.

Naturally, as the days passed, she discovered many things about him. Where he had lived and gone to school. His preferences in food and clothes and decor. His favorite color—blue, as it was for most men. And he learned of her life on the farm: the 4-H calf she had raised and shown at the county fair, winning a second-place ribbon with it; her third-grade teacher who had been mean and scared all the kids by rapping them on the knuckles with a ruler when she was angry.

The days passed swiftly, with a natural cadence to them. Life felt full of harmony to Melba as each one flowed into the next with a seamless joy. It wasn't until Sunday morning of her last week on the island that she realized the hourglass was running out.

She dressed in a sundress, a blue one with tiny yellow flowers printed on the fabric, while she contemplated that fact. Going to the kitchen, she poured her glass of juice and walked outside to stand by the edge of the pool as usual. Roth swam back and forth a few times before coming to the side where she stood. He climbed out with a ripple of smooth muscles.

She smiled at the old pair of cutoffs he was wearing for a bathing suit. They were the ones he had worn the day she had called him a pirate and he had heaved her onto his shoulder in retaliation.

So many memories, she realized. Each day makes its own and then they're gone. Minutes and hours and days sliding past, faster and faster, until you're dizzy and breathless with the hurry of it all. And never a moment to look back and see where you've been. Or to enjoy your accomplishments and triumphs...and your friends.

"What is it?" he asked, lifting the glass from her fingers and drinking from it—another ritual between them now.

"I was just thinking of time and how it passes. This is my last week here. I'll miss Adriane and Glenna and Hattie." She smiled at him. "And you."

He handed her the nearly empty glass. "Maybe we won't let you go. Maybe we'll kidnap you and keep you locked in a secret place, only letting you out when no one is around." His hand caressed along her jaw while his eyes roamed her face possessively.

For one insane moment, she almost believed he would do it. And for an insane second more, she wished he would.

She realized just how vulnerable she was becoming toward him. She was on the brink of falling in love. Maybe she had gone over the edge already. That would be a stupid thing to do. She turned from his hand, her face troubled by thoughts that refused to be suppressed this time.

She now knew why she had resented his presence from the first. He had been a danger to her carefully controlled emotions and to the passionate side of her that she had buried so deep within. With Tom, she had been young and foolish, believing in love and all it promised. This time, if she were hurt, it would be her own fault; this time, she knew the heaven that Roth's eyes promised was an illusion.

Desire was a fleeting thing, a soap bubble, beautiful and iridescent, but it would burst at the first prick of reality. And this fantasy life was nearing an end. Soon she must return to her real world. Already, she knew that she would pay for this idyll in loneliness when the week was over. She had become used to a man's attention and companionship, and she would have to give that up just as she had given up her dreams when Tom had refused to marry her.

She wouldn't fall in love again, she vowed. There was too much pain in it for a woman. With that decision firm in her mind, she nodded when Roth asked if she were ready to go in.

Chapter Eight

Roth was still at the table with Melba when Glenna and Adriane came in. They discussed the general plans for the week.

"Friday night, the Chamber of Commerce is having a dinner at Sea Point. We'll be attending that." He looked at Melba. "What color dress are you going to wear? I want to order the flowers today."

She wasn't sure how formal the dinner was. Turning to Adriane, she asked, "What are you wearing?"

"This isn't a family affair," he told her. "Just you and I are going. Did you bring a long dress?"

She had brought two, at Adriane's insistence. "Wear the sea-green one," the girl advised now. "It brings out the color of your eyes."

But Melba knew her clothes and the effect she wanted. "I think the brown would be better for this occasion."

"Brown?" Roth questioned, not doubting her choice, only confirming the color.

"Brown," she stated firmly. "A sort of taffy color with deep gold lace, sort of tawny. Brassy," she said with a grin lurking in the corners of her mouth.

He pulled her ponytail. "Watch it," he growled. "You're getting as sassy as my niece."

After expressing the proper indignation over this insult, Adriane spoke to her mother. "Greg and I have been invited to a pool party and a cookout this afternoon over on Hilton Head. It starts at four and goes to who-knows-when."

"For you, it's over at midnight, or I turn into a witch," Glenna told her. Speaking generally to the group, she said, "I'm having dinner with friends staying up at North Beach. They have an apartment in one of the condominiums there and have just opened it for the summer."

"In that case, Melba and I will take a picnic dinner over to the little island and explore it this afternoon. There's a low tide between four and five," Roth told them.

Glenna nodded. "Fine. I'll tell Hattie she has the night off. She has a new mystery novel to read, so that will make her happy."

They spent the rest of the morning in quiet activities, reading the Sunday papers before going over to Hilton Head for the church services. Roth accompanied them each Sunday, which was a further revelation to Melba. She thought Adriane's estimate of her uncle as a kind, loving person to be more accurate than Glenna's description of a womanizer parading a harem through his bedroom. Why hadn't he ever married and had children of his own?

Greg came over at three that afternoon. Soon after that, he and Adriane left. Glenna went to her room to rest after a long jogging session on the beach with Melba.

Melba yawned sleepily, wishing she could take a nap, too.

"Come on, woman, off your duff. It's time to raid the refrigerator if we're going to make the low tide," Roth decided, giving her a playful shake to wake her up.

"I'm too tired—all that jogging," she grumbled, but she allowed him to drag her along to the kitchen.

Once there, he rummaged around in the refrigerator, finding roast beef and ham, then he set her to work making sandwiches. "Lots of mustard on mine," he requested. "Lots. And put some of those hot peppers in, too."

"On your sandwich?" she asked.

"No, dummy, wrap them separately," he exclaimed in mock exasperation. "Let's see, potato chips," he mumbled from the depths of the closet pantry.

"I don't like potato chips," she called to him.

He stuck his head out. "What do you mean, you don't like potato chips? They're everyone's favorite junk food."

"Not mine." she asserted. "I eat them once in a while, but I don't really like them. I'll take some dill pickles for me. Do you want any?"

After much arguing over the contents of the picnic basket, they were ready at last. They set out wading across the sandbar, wearing their bathing suits with long-sleeved shirts, jeans, and tennis shoes dangling around their necks. Roth carried the basket in one hand and held Melba's hand with his other. She was glad of his support when she stepped on some un-identified object that moved, causing her to shriek and jump.

''Sissy,'' Roth laughed at her, but she didn't mind. His teasing was like a caress.

In a short time, they were on the little island that was slowly being reabsorbed by the restless sea. It was about three acres in area. A short stretch of beach was accessible on the eastern side of the line of dunes because of the low tide, but Roth headed for the western side of the island.

Leading the way along the narrow apron of sand, he seemed to know exactly where they should go to have their supper, and Melba trailed along beside him, content to follow his guidance.

Her eyes were misty green, catching the light re-flecting from the water and the verdant growth cov-ering the sandy terrain. Scrub oak mingled with sand pine in a random mixture. Here and there, she caught a glimpse of a more exotic bush that indi-cated human habitation at some time. A few birds called back and forth, but they were invisible in the thick foliage.

Although boats skimmed along the Waterway, she had a sense of isolation, as if she had stepped back into some distant time and there was no one but

Roth and herself, silently walking this strange shore together...the only man and the only woman.

At a spot approximately at the midpoint of the island, Roth indicated the remains of a wooden pier. "Let's sit here and put our shoes on before we go into the interior. I think it will hold our weight." He sat on a thick log plank that spanned two huge pilings and dried his feet with a handkerchief before pulling on his socks and shoes. With a wry grimace, he promptly took them off, slid into his jeans, then replaced his footgear while she snickered. "Your turn, smarty," and he ruffled her hair after handing over his handkerchief.

Melba sat on the plank and dried her feet.

"Stay here while I take our picnic basket to a safe place. I don't want to lug it around with us while we explore." He looked at his watch. "It's four o'clock. We have two hours before we have to make it back across the sandbar, or else the water will be too high and the current too swift."

She nodded as he walked off into the lush growth, disappearing almost at once. He was gone just long enough for her to begin to feel apprehensive, then he returned. Her smile of relief was dazzling as she jumped down from the remains of the pier.

He took her hand, his smile lighting his face and her heart. His glance of approval took in her jeans and shoes as he checked her over before leading the way into the island shrubbery. There was a faint but discernible path through the trees, and they followed it for a short distance before coming to a brick rectangle.

"How's your deductive reasoning?" he asked, indicating the man-made structure. "What do you think it is?"

She walked around it, viewing it from all sides, then she examined the inside. A chimney seemed to be the logical conclusion for one end of the rectangle, even though most of it was missing. The bricks were blackened with soot, and that was her clue. A built-in ledge on the inside of the structure could have held a metal grill.

"A barbecue pit," she announced confidently.

He was impressed. "That was good. Or was it just a wild guess?"

She tried to look smugly superior but failed. A wide grin spread over her mouth. "Was I right?"

It was all he could do not to pull her into his arms and kiss her senseless. All the passion he had held in severe restrain for four weeks threatened to break the dam of his self-control. He wasn't sure he could hold out much longer.

Some of his longing must have shown on his face, for the saucy expression was replaced by a somber one as she gazed at him. For a long minute, they stood there, staring at each other, before she turned away, refusing to acknowledge the message in his eyes and in her own suddenly hammering heart.

"I'll give you a brief history," he said in husky tones, forcing to stillness the wild surging within. Time was running out, he realized. This was the last week. "There used to be a summer house here on the island dating from the 1740's. It belonged to a family who had a plantation inland from Charleston.

Then, in the early part of this century, a lodge was built to start a charter boat and fishing business, but it burned to the ground before it was even finished.''

''What happened to the family who owned the plantation?''

''I understand they lost everything in the Civil War. Their sons were killed in battle, the house was burned, and the place was broken up and sold as small farms after the war was over.''

''And the island?''

''Nathaniel Webster bought both islands as one package in 1871. My grandfather, Mason Roth Webster, leased this smaller parcel to the friend who wanted to start the boating business but failed. Since that time, no one has tried to use it for anything except an occasional picnic.''

She glanced around the wooded glen with a nostalgic sadness. ''It's disappearing, isn't it?'' she murmured with a catch in her throat.

''Maybe,'' he agreed. ''The sea and land go through cycles. Right now, the breach between Webster and this island is increasing, but next year, more sand might be dumped along the sandbar, building it up again.''

Her eyes were drawn irresistibly to his as the timbre of his voice changed.

''Who knows how life is going to go?'' he asked quietly. ''We have to take it as it comes. Usually it's sweet, like the summer days we've had lately, but sometimes it's bitter.''

She glanced away from his probing gaze, unable to bear it. Her chest became tight and aching while her emotions went into a tangle. She wished she hadn't come on this outing. Old places and ruins did something to her heart and soul. And so did Roth Webster, she had to admit.

Roth quelled his frustration as she turned from him, hiding the feelings he was sure she was experiencing. He had tried very hard to let her into his life, not pushing her but letting her discover him as a man slowly and through her own perceptions. Surely she knew him well enough now to open herself to him as he had to her.

"Come on," he said. "There's more to see and speculate on. Then we'll eat." He headed off to one side, and she followed, her interest piqued by his enthusiasm.

The land rose into a little hill, and they followed an upward traverse that was very gradual.

"Look." He pointed to the ground. "What do you see?"

She gazed at the spot where a clump of familiar fleshy stalks arched above the wild grass. "Snowdrops!" she said.

Admiration gleamed from his hazel eyes. "Right. And there?"

She followed the line of his finger as he pointed further up the hill. "More snowdrops," she answered.

"Look over there," he indicated behind them.

There was a line of the plants going down the hill in a wide, curving arc, disappearing into a thicket of azaleas. Across the way from them, about six feet, was another clearly visible line of snowdrops, planted parallel to the other curving arc that swept over the hill.

"Why, they were planted!" she exclaimed.

"Very good," he said. "I think this was the road up to the summer house. It went in a long sweeping curve up this incline, then straight at the top to the front door."

"It's narrow for a road," she mused aloud, frowning as she surveyed the evidence.

"Carriages were narrow, but I think they probably only used a pony cart while on the island." He held out a hand. "Come on."

They followed the line of spring-blooming plants. There were gaps in the parallel lines and, at one point, the path diverged into a "Y" shape. Roth thought a little side road led to a glen where a person could sit and rest in solitude while out for a stroll. They explored this possibility and found a small clearing among the tall trees. Returning to the path, they came to another structure, much larger than the pit area.

"This was where the lodge was built. It was to house a restaurant and supplies for the fishermen." Roth stood back and let her explore the ruins.

Melba walked around the perimeter of what had obviously been the foundation for a large square building. The evidence of fire was plain: charred timbers lying at odd angles, blackened bricks scattered all around, some rusty pieces of metal still bearing traces of blistered paint.

Brick columns that had supported the roof of a front porch lay on the ground at equal distance from each other. She counted four of those. A picture of the place took shape in her mind. Carefully, she climbed over the debris and entered the opening of the front door. Roth followed, watching her with a smile curving his lips. She smiled over her shoulder at him as she stepped into the interior of the ruin.

In the center of the large square was a hump of rubble that she puzzled over for several minutes, going around and around it. She tapped her chin while she reviewed the situation. "The floor was here." She measured the distance from the ground with a level hand. "Here was a fireplace, but it was built on top of something." She studied the three arches of brick that rose a few inches from the earth that had been packed around them.

Roth nodded encouragement.

She turned from him and walked slowly around the heap one more time. There was something strangely familiar about those arches. She racked her brain. "Fireplaces!" She whirled on one foot to face Roth. "This fireplace for the lodge was built on top of another fireplace...or something like that. They probably used the existing chimney, and that probably caused the fire. The old structure was unsound. But why three arches?"

"You're doing super, sweetheart. Don't stop now," he said.

"Three fireplaces, back to back? That doesn't make sense," she protested.

"Think about the early plantations. They were afraid of fire, so the kitchens were usually built separately."

"That's it!" she cried. "They built the new lodge on top of the old kitchen ruins. The understructure was an oven and cooking hearths."

He laid his hand on her shoulder. "I'll give you an 'A' for deduction, and since you've done so well, I'll give you a prize."

"What?" she asked, glancing up at him.

"This," he murmured a split-second before his lips touched hers. He schooled himself to patience as he pulled her close, feeling the warm thrust of her breasts against his chest draw an answering warmth from his body. He wondered if she realized just how exciting her body was to him. Her skin was satin smooth, and each time he looked at her, he remembered how lovely she had been, standing on the patio like a dream come to life.

Soon, he thought, she would realize she had been made for him, and then he would touch her all over, tracing out the lines of her breasts, her waist, the convex curve of her hips, the tapering columns of her silken thighs. He lifted his mouth from her soft lips, his breath sounding loud in the silence of the woods.

"I could kiss you all day," he murmured, "but then we wouldn't see the best part of the island." Taking her hand, he led her on along the overgrown path. "The camellia garden," he announced in a moment, waving a hand toward a forest of small trees.

Melba, shaken by the brief kiss, was silent as they walked through the trees. She noted that the camellias had been laid out in straight lines. There were empty spaces where some had died, but most grew in a stately procession, well over their heads.

After that came a lane of crepe myrtles. She realized the lovely flowering trees must be over two hundred years old. "I feel humble and temporary next to these," she told Roth in a low voice.

He smoothed a strand of hair off her forehead. "Yes," he said, understanding. "Our lives must be carried forward through our children." His smile was tender when her gaze flashed from the trees to him. He turned her, continuing on their walk that opened onto a broader avenue when they left the trees. Evidence of a wide lawn stretched on either side of them, and before them, in the soft rays of the setting sun, were the ruins of the summer house.

Her arm through his, they silently climbed the front steps, which had weathered and broken off in layers the way slate fractures. The same material formed walkways all around the foundation of brick and, at the side of the house, made up a patio where one could sit and watch the sunset at the end of the day.

"Hungry?" Roth wanted to know, going to an old live oak at the end of the patio. The picnic basket hung from a limb.

She nodded, not taking her eyes from the ruins. She looked at the remains of walls and fireplaces, trying to decide what each room had been used for. "How many rooms were there?" she asked.

"Not many," he replied, spreading a blanket on the huge blocks of slate. "A living room, dining room, and bedrooms for the adults on the lower level. A sleeping loft for children and servants on the upper one. Did you notice the tabby?''

"A cat?'' She looked around.

"No, tabby is a sort of mortar made of ground oyster shells. It was used to form a stucco finish on many of these old houses. Look at the bricks over there.''

She dutifully examined a section of outside wall while he laid out their sandwiches. He poured each of them a paper cup of lemonade. "Ready,'' he called.

After the meal, Melba lounged back on her elbows. "That was lovely. Thank you for bringing me,'' she said sincerely. Her words put him in the position of host and reminded her of her own position in his household. She had a tendency to forget when they were alone together.

His eyes roamed moodily down her slender frame. It was getting close to time to start back, but he was reluctant to go. He glanced at the ruins. "It's easy to imagine the house as it must have been just before the Civil War, isn't it?''

She nodded slowly, noticing the way the fading light softened the shadows around them, giving the scene an ethereal beauty. The silence was intense, and the trembling of the leaves in the slight ocean breeze was like fairy music, barely heard.

Her voice, when she spoke, was hushed. "I can almost feel the silk dress with the hooped petticoat under it that I would be wearing in those times. I'm sitting here on the patio, watching the sun set across the water toward the mainland. Maybe dreaming about my beau, who is coming over from Webster or Hilton Head or even up from Savannah.''

Roth watched her eyes go misty as she became lost in her dream. He ate the rest of a chocolate chip cookie, washed it down with lemonade, then stood and walked off a few paces. Turning to her questioning glance, he straightened an imaginary cravat, walked toward her and bowed elegantly from the waist.

"Good evening, Miss Holly. Captain Roth Webster at your service," he announced himself, speaking in a soft drawl.

"Captain Webster," she greeted him, inclining her head in a gracious but demure manner. "How delightful to see you." She rose gracefully, pretending to smooth her silk skirts over her petticoats, and executed a perfect curtsy. Fluttering her lashes, she remarked, "Hasn't it been a lovely day?"

His eyes darkened to forest green as they swept over her jeans and shirt as if she were indeed wearing the finest silks. "Mighty lovely, ma'am, mighty lovely," he agreed, never taking his eyes from her.

The intensity of his gaze flustered her poise. She turned from him with a real blush highlighting her cheeks. "And how is your dear sister? I understand she and her daughter are visiting with you?" she continued with their make-believe.

He was directly behind her when he spoke. "Yes. They send their regards and their regrets for missing your ball this evening. They had prior commitments."

She moved forward a couple of feet before saying with a gay little laugh, "I quite understand."

Going out of character, she whirled several dancing steps across the patio tiles. "It must have been wonderful, going to a ball in those days. Ball gowns of silk and satin, exquisite lace and ribbons adorning every edge. Handsome escorts in elegant evening clothes. Black boots, silk ties, oh, and those tall beaver hats. Horses and carriages and footmen."

She half closed her eyes, seeing the scene in her mind. Her hands were out at her sides as if she held wide skirts under control, and her slender body swayed back and forth to the music of invisible violins.

Roth held out his hand. "Miss Holly, would you do me the honor of this dance?" he asked in formal tones.

Before she could answer, he took her into his arms. His hand rested lightly at her waist, the other outstretched to hold hers in the correct manner. He began to waltz, humming a melody softly as he moved her about the patio.

It seemed so natural to her, so much a part of their setting that, sighing blissfully, she closed her eyes and let the magic have its way with her. Gradually, she was drawn closer until her cheek nestled against his chest.

Into the twilight they danced in their private ball. The world could have ended, and neither would have noticed. Their steps slowed until they forgot to move and simply stood, swaying gently like flowers caressed by the breeze.

Roth's hand left her waist to curl under her jaw, lifting her head from its resting place. For a long minute, they looked into each other's eyes. Then he kissed her.

It was a grave kiss, serious and meaningful. It asked and demanded at the same time. Passion was part of it but not all. He raised his head and again they gazed into each other's eyes. He smiled slightly at what he saw in hers.

Then his lips parted hers and the embrace deepened. His tongue caressed hers with sensuous stroking and probing touches. Be gentle, he reminded himself. With her, he wanted to be.

A pressure formed in her chest as if something inside her were trying to break free of its bindings. It hurt, and behind her closed eyes, tears formed. She felt as if she were being torn into shreds. She held him closer, binding her wounds with his healing warmth.

Roth knew something of the agony she was going through. He could feel it in the trembling of her mouth under his, in the tightening desperation of her arms around his shoulders. He prayed that she was emerging from her protective shell and that she was ready to come to him as an equal, his partner in passion and in life…woman, warm and willing, giving fully of herself.

"I want you," he murmured in husky tones. "God, I want you. Don't be afraid to come to me." His hands stroked her back, and he moved his legs, widening his stance to form a welcoming cove for her to shelter in. She stepped forward into his total embrace, and he exulted in the act of faith on her part.

Melba accepted his protection like a kitten taking refuge beside a trusted canine friend. He was the most compellingly masculine man she had ever known, yet she instinctively knew that he would never use force on her. He didn't have Tom's gentleness, yet she knew he wouldn't hurt her, that he would guard her from the strength of his passion.

This time her passion wasn't the erupting of a volcano, but the consuming flames of a steadily increasing fire. Did she want that consummation? Could she stop it? she wondered.

When he lifted her in his arms and carried her to the blanket, she simply held on until he carefully laid her down, then lay down beside her.

His fingers spread over her tummy just below her breasts, caressing her skin in little kneading strokes while he gazed his fill of her. His eyes burned with a glow like foxfire, lighting her to her very depths. It was as if he were already inside her, part of her, his spirit joined to hers.

He unfastened his shirt and hers, his lean, strong fingers moving with skill at the task. He folded them together and made a pillow which he slipped under her head. He removed the modest white bra of her swimming suit and laid it aside. Then he gazed with unconcealed adoration at her breasts.

He formed his fingers into a tiny cup and covered the tip of one nipple, then he let his fingers open while sliding his hand forward so that the entire globe was captured in his hand. Her nipple rose to meet his palm, and he laughed softly, pleased with the reaction.

"I'll never get enough of you. When I look at your lips, I'm reminded of your breasts; when I look at your breasts, I remember your lips." His chest moved in silent laughter. "Then I can't decide which I want to kiss the most."

He kissed her breasts, then moved back to her mouth. His kisses rained on her chin and nose and eyes, all over her face. He searched her neck and throat and found all the sensitive spots.

Letting his body roll partially on hers, he captured her legs beneath one of his. Writhing beneath him, she brought him to the brink of abandon. He let his body close over her, and he stroked every inch of her with the pressing of his hard male frame—chest to chest, hip to hip, thigh to thigh.

Melba ran her hands along the smooth, flexing muscles of his back. She stroked his hair and caressed him along the powerful cords of his neck. She marveled at the strength evident in his arms when she touched the rock-hard muscles of his biceps.

She reveled in the warmth that poured over her from him. She kissed the wiry hairs of his chest, seeking the skin beneath with her tongue, drawing damp circles of desire there that wrenched a ragged sigh from him.

"Melba. Sweetheart," he whispered in shaken tones that indicated the depth of his ardor. "You're a wild, sweet fruit, and I could live off the honey of your kisses for days." His stormy gaze took on a teasing light, invading the passionate fire of his eyes as he lessened the tempest that raged between them.

She stroked the thick mass of curls that were the color of autumn leaves with summer's golden glow still in them. Her fingers trailed along his back, the tips following the indentation of his spine, until they reached his jeans. Impatient with the cloth that prevented contact with his flesh, she pulled at the fabric, mindlessly wanting it out of the way.

Roth abruptly moved from her, throwing himself on his back with an arm shielding his face. His chest lifted and fell as he sucked in deep gulps of air.

Like a child reaching for that which it instinctively wants, her hand reached for him, caressing his skin through the mat of hair. He rolled back to her, his weight a welcome addition to her own. She sighed and moved against him, snuggling closer.

"Who am I?" he demanded hoarsely.

Opening her eyes, she stared blankly at him.

"Who am I?" His hand tightened at her waist.

She understood the words but not the question. She shook her head slightly, not comprehending what he was asking.

"Are you kissing me or Tom? Is it my arms that hold you or are you pretending that I'm him?" he asked harshly.

She recoiled from the charge. "No!"

"You called me by his name before. Say my name. Say it!"

"Roth," she said, barely above a whisper. "Roth."

"Yes," he groaned, "yes."

Gathering her to him, he kissed her fiercely, passionately, with something akin to desperation in his touch. She didn't understand what he wanted from her, but she felt his longing and tried to soothe him with her embrace.

Finally, he released her mouth. "You're not to think of him when I kiss you," he muttered savagely.

"I don't," she told him. "I wasn't calling you by his name the other time. It was just that you made me feel so different. You're much more aggressive than Tom and...and I started to tell you, but you took offense."

"You were still thinking of him, comparing our techniques," he accused, but he no longer sounded angry. He was silent for a long time as he held her and gazed into her eyes as if he would find her very soul. "Do you still resent me?" he asked softly.

"I don't know," she confessed honestly. Now that she understood the basis of her earlier feelings, she could no longer sustain them, but neither did she want to succumb to them. She closed her eyes against his scrutiny. "I don't know what I feel anymore."

"Well," he breathed against her ear, "that's a start." He seemed pleased all at once. He began nibbling on her earlobe, sending electricity down her neck.

"Roth, don't," she pleaded. She pushed at him.

"Why not?" he asked with male logic.

"This isn't right."

He lifted his head. "You're wrong," he said quietly. "This is the one thing between us that is."

She moved her head slowly back and forth, then faster as her resolve built. "No. I'm here as a professional. There can be nothing more."

He looked at her in frustration. "What are you talking about?"

"I'm a nurse, and I'm employed by your sister in that capacity," she explained. "I go into people's homes during times of stress and illness. I can't take advantage of the situation."

"You're hardly taking advantage," he murmured, chuckling. "I wish you would. You want me and I want you...very much...more than I've ever wanted anything in my life. You must believe that."

She fought with her conscience over his persuasive comments. "A person can't just take what he wants from life," she lectured. "I have a responsibility to Adriane."

"Adriane has nothing to do with this," Roth said sternly. "She isn't here. This is between the two of us, a man and a woman who have been involved from the moment we met, whether you want to admit that or not." Softening, he stroked her hair back from her forehead. "You're off-duty now, little one. Be a woman, my woman," he urged huskily.

He lowered his head and kissed her as though she were a fragile, bruisable delicacy, but even as he tried to be gentle with her, the embrace deepened of its own accord. They were too volatile together, his flesh igniting hers, hers inflaming his.

Her arms slipped around his neck, fingers seeking

the wind-tangled curls of his hair. She opened her mouth to him, loving the taste of him on her tongue, the texture of his lips on hers.

Groaning deep in his throat, he eased their bodies into more comfortable positions on the hard slate. Her body answered his passion, becoming ever more yielding, more pliable to his touch. "You're wonderful, delicious," he whispered, bestowing little love bites along her neck.

"You're so warm. You make me come alive again, as if I had been asleep. But now I'm awake." She spoke in ragged phrases as his touch became more demanding.

"Yes," he murmured urgently. "Warm, alive, awake." His head dipped to her breasts. He mouthed each pointed tip, bringing laughter and gasping exclamations to her throat, then sighing ecstasy as his tongue transcribed fiery messages of passionate need over her flesh. "Oh, love, you feel so good to me."

She heard the one word…*love*. An infinite sadness pierced her heart. This wasn't love; it was only the passion of this moment, of this time and place. She was merely a role model for Adriane, and the mindless joy of being in his arms was a foolish fantasy, one that she shouldn't allow. An unbidden tear rolled down each of her cheeks, wetting his face as he sought her lips. "I can't. Roth, I can't," she whispered, frightened at the degree of longing that rose in her, matching the desire in him.

Roth stopped pressing her with kisses as he realized the reality of the pain in her. He crushed her to him, making small sounds of comfort, not understanding her hurt but feeling the need she had for something more than passion. He stifled his own disappointment. She still didn't trust him enough to come to him. What if she never did? He refused to think about that.

"You and your scruples," he mocked her gently, putting them back on the professional level, one that she could handle. "Next week," he warned her, teasing yet serious, "that won't be the case. You'll be through here, and then there'll be nothing to keep me from you. Do you realize that?" He gave her a little squeeze, demanding an acknowledgement from her.

"I'm sorry. You must think I'm the worst sort of wishy-washy person," she said shakily, moving from him and drying her eyes. She put her clothing back on. "Shouldn't we be getting back?"

"We've missed the tide," he told her, watching her reaction carefully. "I guess I've gotten you into a mess, and I'm sorry for that." He moved his shoulders in an apologetic way.

"It was as much my fault as yours." She hastened to take part of the blame. After all, she had gotten as involved in their passionate embraces as he.

"No, I shouldn't have started that dancing business. I knew better than to take you in my arms."

"I could have refused," she insisted.

He reached over and tweaked her nose. "Are we going to fight over whose fault this is?"

Their eyes met and they suddenly grinned. Laughing, he picked up his shirt and put it on.

Sobering, she glanced around. "Will we have to

spend the night?'' She wasn't sure she could hold out against her own wants and needs for a whole night.

"Yes, until the next low tide in the early morning." He hesitated, then, "Don't worry, love. What's between us will keep, so you can hang on to your principles."

She pondered his words while he got out the rest of the cookies and shared them with her. He was extraordinarily understanding of her inner doubts and fears. From the first, he'd known when to withdraw, when to protect, when to reassure.

Settling beside him on the blanket with her elbows propped on her knees, she asked, "Roth, have you ever been in love? Perhaps when you were in college? Did you ever live with a woman?"

He maintained a solemn outer composure, but inside, he was glad of her question. He thought that it was a good sign that she was interested in his former love life, and he hoped it meant she was also interested in his present one.

"Once, in my first year of college, I met someone. We were in love, I thought."

"What happened?" She felt an immediate sympathy for him.

"I don't know," he said slowly. "At first, we were very happy together, but she didn't want to get married right then. She was establishing herself in her career. I was doing the same. Later, it seemed we had no time for each other; other things always interfered. When she was offered a promotion that would take her to the West Coast, she accepted."

"And that was it? You didn't see each other again."

He shrugged. "A couple of times. But no romance can work forever at long distance."

"And you never met anyone else?" she persisted.

He chuckled. "Are you worried about my advancing age as Adriane appears to be?"

"Well," she drawled suggestively, then burst out laughing at his pained expression.

"You're as bad as my niece," he complained, pulling her to her feet and throwing an arm over her shoulders. "Come on, help an old man take an evening stroll." He guided her away from the picnic area and toward the beach.

It was only later, after they had waded along the moonstruck shore, then returned to their blanket, that she realized he had adroitly turned the conversation into other channels. Yawning, she snuggled into his chest when he folded the scant cover over them. Strangely, she felt better, knowing he had loved before…and knowing his first love was a continent away.

Chapter Nine

"Wake up, love."

Roth spoke near her ear. Melba pushed closer to the heavenly warmth at her side. Her bed felt hard as a rock. It was a rock, she realized, coming fully awake and looking into his amused eyes.

He unwrapped the thin picnic blanket from them and helped her to her feet. "It should be low tide. We have to go."

"All right," she mumbled, stretching stiff muscles and yawning.

The sky was barely light. The time of the false dawn, she thought, following Roth as he led the way back to the beach and then north along the shore to the tip of the little island. The water was knee-deep, sluicing through the channel with a rushing sound.

"Take your shoes off and roll your pants legs up. It won't matter if they get wet since we'll be home soon." He set the basket down and started on the task. When they were ready, he clasped her hand, gave her an encouraging smile, and started across with her in tow.

She hung back, her sleepy eyes riveted on the eastern sky. At that moment, a drop of liquid gold appeared on the horizon. She stopped walking and pointed. "Look, Roth, the sun is rising."

They watched as the drop became a golden arch, growing wider and wider at the edge of the earth.

"Morning," he said, announcing the fact to her and to a trio of seagulls that wheeled overhead.

They continued their journey over the sandbar, then along the beach of Webster Island, and finally over the steps bridging the sand dunes. No one was up, and the doors were locked. Roth knew where a key was hidden and showed it to her. They tiptoed into the house like a couple of sneak-thieves.

At her bedroom door, he whispered, "Thanks for sharing the adventure without grumbling." With a swift kiss, he went down the hall and turned at his door. "Breakfast in thirty minutes," he called back in soft tones.

Hurrying into her room, she removed her damp, wrinkled clothing and dashed into the shower. In the alloted half-hour, she was ready to go to the kitchen.

Roth had English muffins in the toaster and scrambled eggs in a skillet when she entered. He looked as fresh as the morning in dark slacks and a light-blue shirt. He beamed approval at her appearance in yellow pants and a white top with yellow rickrack edging the short sleeves. Her hair was tied in a yellow ribbon at the back of her neck.

They were still at the table when Glenna and Adriane came in. Hattie had been in, looked at the dining couple in surprise, and gone back to her room, shaking her head.

"The least you could have done was call the Coast Guard," Roth said to his sister when she and Adriane were seated.

"What for?" she asked, startled at this strange request.

"Melba and I were stranded for the entire night on the other island and not a soul came looking for us," he elaborated.

Melba wondered if she looked as stunned as she felt. There had been no need to broadcast their disaster. No one would have known if he had kept quiet.

Glenna looked from one to the other. "You appear to be in good health after your ordeal," she commented with a slight sardonic emphasis on the last word.

"We're fine," Roth affirmed. "Luckily, we had the picnic blanket to wrap up in. We got up at dawn, crossed the sandbar at low tide, and came home to a locked house." His aggrieved expression would have done credit to a martyr.

Melba was tempted to borrow from Adriane's mannerisms and give him a swift kick under the table. She hid her face by sipping from her coffee cup for a long time. Roth stood, stretched and yawned luxuriously, then announced he had work to do. With a touch on her shoulder, he ambled off to his study, leaving her to face the other two women on her own.

"Nothing happened," she blurted defensively as they looked at her—Adriane eager, Glenna amused—and then she blushed a furious red.

Glenna frowned at her giggling daughter before touching Melba's arm briefly in a reassuring manner. "We know that." She smiled wryly. "It didn't cross my mind for an instant that you would behave with less than propriety. Now about my brother..."

As Glenna's voice trailed off, Melba wanted to protest the suggestive reference to Roth. If he had pressed only a bit, he could have easily overcome her personal scruples, but he hadn't. "He was very kind," she said solemnly. "And he apologized for getting me into a mess."

More than that, she wasn't going to say. What had happened between them on the island was a personal thing which she wasn't going to share. However, she did have a thing or two to say to her talkative companion in private!

Glenna and Adriane seemed satisfied with her defense of Roth, and the conversation drifted to past picnics they had had, some on that island, some on Webster, and others in Charleston. They went for their morning swim, had lunch, and then took a nap. Roth remained in his study; it was several hours before Melba got a moment alone with him.

She found him in the library when she came out of her room shortly before dinner. "Why did you say anything about last night?" she demanded indignantly.

"I thought it was better to have it out in the open," he said easily. "Would you rather have it slip out at an inopportune time and sound as if we had done something wrong?"

She frowned. "No, but there was no need to blurt it out. I told them that nothing happened between us." Heat flowed up her neck into her cheeks.

"Thank you," he said, keeping a straight face.

She wet her dry lips. "But I think Glenna thinks that you...that you...that I...I just wish you hadn't said anything!"

He ignored her stumbling statement. "I won't have anything clandestine between us. Besides, it can hardly be a secret that I want you, when I'm pursuing you in full sight of my family," he told her in reasonable tones. "And with their approval."

The remainder of the week passed much as the previous two had. Roth was entirely open in his regard for her; he wasn't suggestive around his family, but he didn't hide his interest, either. Adriane watched them with stars in her eyes while Glenna seemed amused by the situation.

Melba admitted that his attention was devastating, and she reminded herself often that he was doing this for Adriane. Not entirely, of course. She believed that he really did find her desirable, but she didn't fool herself that this was more than a summer's entertainment for him, different from his usual affairs since this wasn't that deeply involved, but still, an affair of sorts.

On Thursday afternoon, Roth left for Charleston

to take care of some business, promising to return early the next day. His eyes lingered on Melba as he said good-bye at the pier.

On Friday morning, Melba got up at the usual time and went to the deck over the sand dunes to watch the sunrise. Birds ran behind each receding wave to snatch their breakfast in the shallows. With the familiar squeezing sensation catching her breath, she wondered what time Roth would be home today. She missed him this morning, she admitted. She had grown accustomed to their quiet times together.

At eight o'clock, Hattie and Glenna came into the kitchen where she was eating cereal. They discussed the menu for dinner.

Adriane bounced in. "Don't forget, Uncle Roth and Melba are going out tonight," she reminded her mother.

"Oh, that's right," Glenna said. They changed the menu to a simpler one, then changed their minds completely and decided to go over to Sea Point for the buffet.

"I'm glad we got that settled," Hattie declared, nodding her head. Her gray hair had recently been permed into a fluff of fresh curls around her face, and she had taken to wearing a bit of color on her lips.

All of them pitched in on the housework, and at a few minutes before ten, Melba, Glenna, and Adriane dived into the pool together and started their daily exercise routine. Hattie brought her book out and hiked her skirt two inches above her knees. Adriane teased the housekeeper with a wolf whistle.

The three bathers swam and then tossed a Frisbee back and forth across the pool. Spreading towels on the grass, they lay in the sun to dry. Melba was alert for the sounds of a boat's motor, although she knew she probably wouldn't hear it from here unless the wind was from that direction. Which it wasn't.

After a while, Hattie went in to prepare lunch. Adriane and Melba decided they wanted some lemonade to tide them over and went in, too. Glenna took another swim before the noon meal. She dived into the pool alone. The two younger women, wearing towel sarongs, brought the pitcher of icy drink out to the picnic table on the lower patio along with three glasses.

"I'll call Mom if she hasn't drowned by now." Adriane issued this cheerful message while Melba poured the lemonade. Adriane turned and stopped in her tracks, her face going pale.

Alerted by the girl's unusual behaviour, Melba's professional gaze checked her over. "What is it, Adriane?" she asked quietly.

"Shh," the girl said. Her eyes were riveted on the upper patio.

Melba turned toward the pool level, not knowing what to expect but prepared for anything. A strange man stood just outside the library door. He, too, was staring at the swimming pool, as frozen in his posture as Adriane appeared to be.

He was in his forties, Melba guessed, and dressed in an expensive summer suit of light gray. He had a brisk, neat appearance and was handsome with gray touches in his dark hair. He looked distinguished and well-to-do.

She tried to remember if she had seen him at the resort during the many times she had gone over there. Was he a business associate of Roth's? But that didn't explain Adriane's reaction to him. Her face wore a look of utter vulnerability.

"Glenna?" he said in a strained voice.

There was a moment of tense silence. Adriane caught Melba's arm. "Daddy," she mouthed, eyes wide with shock.

In what must have been a miracle of self-control, Glenna laughed lightly. "Oops, caught," she commented. "Hello, Bruce, come on in, the water's fine."

A splash rained on the pavement, and Bruce Langdon stepped back automatically. Then he walked forward to the edge of the pool.

"Hand me my robe, will you?" Glenna asked. She climbed up the ladder and stood dripping on the patio. Her youthful body was an even golden tan all over. The blond hair curled damply around her shoulders. She wrung out the excess water with a casual air, then shook her head to loosen the strands once more.

For a long beat of time, her husband didn't move, but in a moment, drawing a visible breath, he picked up the robe and held it while Glenna slipped her arms into the sleeves and tied the sash around her narrow waist.

"What are you doing here?" she asked conversationally.

"I have some papers for you to sign." He gestured vaguely behind him.

"Let's go into the library, shall we?" She led the way, regal in every line of her body. He followed, still dazed.

Adriane whirled to Melba. "I wish...I wish..." she whispered desperately. Burying her face against Melba, she cried silently, tremors shaking her slender body.

"I know, love, but wishing doesn't make it happen," Melba told her gently. "We can only make things happen in our own lives. Other people have to work things out for themselves."

She looked over the streaky blond hair to meet hazel eyes gazing at her from the kitchen door. The intensity of Roth's stare willed her to confront the meaning of her words in relation to herself.

Something buried deep in the most secret part of her contracted suddenly, painfully, bringing a blinding stab of light with it, striking her with brilliance as she realized she loved this man totally, with everything in her, more than she had ever loved before.

She wanted to look away but couldn't. Roth wouldn't let her. He captured her gaze with his own darkly glowing one and refused to let it go. The distance between them crackled with visual questions that flashed from him to her.

The painful sensation left her, crowded out by the filling of her senses with Roth...Roth...her teasing pirate, her gentleman officer. She had resented his intrusion into the orderliness of her life, reviving the feelings she had tried to deny, but he, with his vitality and determination, had broken through her every defense.

Her face must have mirrored some of her emotions as her heart glowed white-hot with new life. His face relaxed, and his eyes ran over her in possessive promise before he quietly retreated into the house.

Adriane raised her tear-stained face. "I know," she admitted. "I'm okay now." She smiled then, and Melba's heart overflowed with love for this young girl and her courage. And for all this family, she realized.

Melba smoothed on deep brown shadow, added a golden line of highlighter beneath her eyebrow, then stroked mascara along her naturally dark lashes. She used her favorite mauve lipstick that deepened her lip color without making her lips look painted.

The chocolate-taffy brown of her dress enhanced the tawny gold shades of her hair, which fell over her shoulders to mingle with the deep gold of the lace trim. Gold sandals and purse completed her ensemble.

Her shapely arms were visible through the sheer, fluttering fabric of the long sleeves, and the swell of her breasts loomed modestly over the rounded neckline frothed with gold lace. Draping a sweater over her arm, she went to the library to wait for Roth. He was already there.

"If anyone tries to tell me that brown isn't the sexiest color in the world, I'll call him a liar," he murmured, pinning a corsage of roses with fluffy

gold petals to the top of her dress. "You're beautiful."

"Thank you," she managed to say. She fought a
strong impulse to wrap her arms around his neck
and urge his lips to hers in order to ease the hunger
he aroused in her.

Her entire body tingled as he led her down the
path and helped her into the boat a few minutes
later. The other three women and Bruce Langdon
had gone over earlier in Roth's yacht, leaving the
rental one for the couple. Melba thought of Glenna
and Bruce as Roth piloted them over the channel.

The estranged pair had spent several hours in the
library alone that afternoon. Now he was going to
spend a few days at the island. Melba sensed a rec-
onciliation in the air. For Adriane's sake, she hoped
so. A grin pushed its way onto her lips. Bruce had
certainly received a shock upon finding his lovely
wife swimming in the nude, and Glenna had carried
off the scene wonderfully. Melba had been proud of
both mother and daughter's poise and naturalness
during the rest of the day.

When they reached the resort, Roth tossed her
sweater to the receptionist to keep until they were
ready to leave. They spoke to Nigel and Shirl, who
were going into the formal dining room as they went
toward the banquet room.

Melba couldn't help being filled with pride at the
quickly smothered glare from the gorgeous model.
Roth drew her hand into the crook of his arm, and
she let herself cling, just a little, to him.

"How lovely you're looking this evening," Shirl

said with just the right amount of warmth. "That dress is simply perfect for someone with your color tones."

Roth cut in smoothly. "If you'll excuse us, we're a little late." He guided Melba into the private room that had been reserved for the Chamber of Commerce dinner.

For the next half hour, she stayed close to Roth while he introduced her to a score of people, then chatted pleasantly with them until it was time to eat. To her consternation, they were seated at the head table, but his smile was so reassuring that she got over her nerves.

As the evening progressed, she enjoyed herself more and more. The matronly lady next to her turned out to be a banker who explained her work in high finance in a clearly comprehensible manner. She glanced over once to find Roth watching her with an indulgent smile curving his sensuous lips. She returned it tenfold.

After the main course, the waiters removed the dishes and served the dessert.

"Did you plan this?" she demanded of Roth when strawberry shortcake was placed in front of her.

"No, but I wish I had," he said with an intimate chuckle. His gaze held hers for a second before he picked up his spoon and scooped a plump strawberry into his mouth.

Her skin tingled with hidden fire at his action and at the play of his seductive eyes over her. She concentrated on her treat for several minutes before looking at him again.

She was thankful for the after-dinner coffee before the speeches began. There were several, for it was an awards night, and everyone who received one had to say a few words, including Roth. She applauded demurely with the rest when he sat down, but she wanted to clap like mad.

Finally, it was over and they said their farewells. Excusing herself, she went into the ladies' lounge to repair her makeup. Roth told her he would be in the office and to meet him there when she was finished.

The receptionist smiled brightly and pointed out the door when Melba asked for directions a few minutes later.

Melba went through a door marked ''Private'' and stood in a short hall with four doors, one of which spilled light into the dim hallway. She approached the opening with an anticipatory smile on her lips and stars in her eyes, reflecting her inner happiness.

Roth's voice halted her. She recognized the tone as one she had heard him use with Glenna that first day at Webster Island. His voice was cool, patient, and controlled, but a hardness like granite underscored the gentler modulations.

''But that is the way it is. I'm with her because I *want* to be with her.'' His tone gentled suddenly. ''Does that explain how I feel?''

''Yes, darling, I think it does,'' Shirl answered with admirable composure, a tinkling little laugh highlighting the words.

Roth moved into view, gazing past Shirl to see Melba hesitating on the threshold. A smile lit his eyes, but before he could speak, Melba laid a finger over her lips and silently withdrew. She wouldn't embarrass Shirl with her presence at this moment, although she was sure the model would handle her appearance with aplomb if faced with the situation. Melba was filled with pity for her.

She went back to the lobby. Like a refrain, Adriane's words came back to her: Once Uncle Roth is through with a woman, he's through forever. She applied those words to herself. Her duties here as a nurse were finished, and Roth had made it clear he was only waiting until that moment. And then? Then nothing would stand in the way of their affair. And after that? she relentlessly asked. After that, when he tired of her, he would go back to his life, and she would be left to endure the hurt alone. She couldn't go through that again. She couldn't. It would be much worse this time for she loved Roth more, with the deep, aching love that comes from experience and the revival of hopes that shouldn't have been revived at all. She fought the tears that threatened to fall.

A hand on her arm forced her to regain her slipping control. The face she turned to Nigel was as composed as Shirl Bard's had ever been. "Hello, Nigel," she said calmly.

"How was the dinner?" he asked.

"Fine." How long could she carry on this inane conversation? She wished Shirl and Roth would finish burying their old affair. Was Shirl perhaps cry-

ing? She saw the answer to that question was no as
Shirl and Roth came through the door and across the
lobby to her and Nigel.

Roth's smile was its usual devastating one. He
and Shirl could have just spent a pleasant few
minutes talking of the weather. Melba marveled at
their acting ability. "Ready to go?" he asked, his
eyes going over her with hunger in their depths.

They forgot her sweater, and on the way back to
the island, she sat next to him with his jacket around
her shoulders to keep warm. A tremor started somewhere inside her and spread to her limbs rapidly. At
the house, where all was quiet, he followed her into
her room, turning her into his arms before she could
protest.

His lips met hers with tender abandon, driving all
sane thought from her mind. His hands urged her to
wild, willing response. The precarious tears rose to
the surface again as his mouth roamed her face, always returning to the sweetness of her mouth.

"Come with me," he said. "Your tour of duty
was officially over at five o'clock today. Now you
belong to me." His smile wrapped around her heart,
filling her with breathless longing. "Come to my
room now, love, and be with me."

"I think it would be better if I didn't," she said,
the tremor in her body invading her voice. She
couldn't go with him. It would be worse than foolish
to do so, she warned her yearning heart. But she
wanted to so much. She wanted all the promises that
his eyes had given, the passion his touch had in-

duced, the ecstasy his voice had conveyed. Oh, yes, she wanted everything!

"Why?" he asked lazily, his head bending until his lips could caress along her cheek. He inhaled deeply. "You smell delicious."

"Roth, please." She pushed lightly at his chest as his arms tightened around her.

He lifted his head. "What is this?" he asked quietly.

"Nothing," she insisted. And that was what it was going to remain between them, she vowed. Nothing.

"You're retreating into your shell again." His frown filled her with dread. It would take so little to change his passion to anger. But maybe she could handle that better than the passion.

"Don't be ridiculous. I'm tired, and I want to go to bed...alone. I have to pack tomorrow and then drive home."

His fingers dug into her shoulders. "I can't believe this. What happened to the warm, laughing woman I've come to know during this past three weeks? What happened to the friendship we've shared? Doesn't that mean anything? What's happened to send you scurrying for cover again?"

"N-nothing," she stuttered.

"Was it the conversation with Shirl? Didn't you hear me tell her how I felt about you?"

He gave her a little shake when she didn't answer right away. Slowly, she nodded.

"Well?" he demanded. "Surely you know there's no woman in my life but you." His voice dropped to seductive levels. "Haven't I been patient, letting you have your way, even though I've hardly slept in weeks for thinking of you? Don't I deserve a reward for good behavior?" he cajoled, nearly melting her resistance with the sweetness of it.

"You have been patient," she told him. "And sweet. And kind. I really appreciate it. We've had a lovely interlude." She stopped, found the courage for the last part and said, "But now it's over. I'll be busy, and of course, you'll be involved in your businesses."

It was the hardest thing she had ever done, to smile and meet his gaze and hold it against his anger and disbelief, but she did it. Abruptly, he let her go and walked out, slamming the door behind him.

Chapter Ten

"Here's the extra prints of the pictures I've taken while you've been here," Adriane said the next morning as Melba prepared to leave. She stuck them into Melba's open purse. "Mom and Dad are making up, I think," she whispered as if afraid to say the magic words aloud.

"It would be great if they did, wouldn't it?" Melba whispered back. "Well, that's it," she said in normal tones as she closed her last suitcase. "Are you going to take me over?"

Adriane frowned. "I suppose. Uncle Roth is gone in his boat, but we have the rental one." She bit on her bottom lip, obviously wanting to ask more but unsure how her questions would be received.

Melba decided she should say something to ease her young friend's mind and settle the question about her and Roth for all time. "I don't know when I've had a nicer time with a patient. You're like family to me. Roth reminds me of my brother back home—teasing and full of fun. Both of them can be devils at times." She grimaced in exaggerated amusement and was gratified by Adriane's answering laughter.

Adriane helped carry the luggage, waiting at the door while Melba said good-bye to Hattie, Glenna, and Bruce, then they set off in the yacht. At Sea Point, Greg was waiting for them. He helped her stow her things in the compact auto, then gave her a kiss of farewell and handed her the extra set of car keys.

The hardest part was saying good bye to Adriane. They simply stood for a moment, their arms around each other, then Melba got in the car.

"Don't forget." Adriane leaned her head down to the window to speak. "You're to come back here for a week after your next case." Her look was entreating, her eyes filled with unshed tears.

"We'll see," Melba temporized. "Regardless, I'll see you in Charleston in August." She backed out, waved, and started home.

At noon, she pulled into her driveway and, stretching wearily, went into her apartment. Mrs. Wilkins had already been in. The place was aired and dusted. A note on the kitchen counter invited Melba to supper that night.

Her lips trembled into an affectionate smile. She wasn't sure she would be very good company. Tears pressed constantly against her eyes, which, con-

versely, felt hot and dry. Emotion was a funny thing,
she thought.

Very profound, she mocked, opening her purse
and dropping her car keys inside. She noticed the
packet of photos and slowly withdrew them. She
opened the envelope and looked…and looked…at
the smiling faces.

The one she looked at the longest was the one of
Roth standing on the pier in his cutoffs with his
hands on his hips. Carrying it, she went into her
bedroom. Lifting the frame, she slid Tom's picture
out and placed Roth's in the center, then pushed the
photo back into place under the glass.

It came to her in a moment of truth that she had
never forgiven Tom for destroying her dreams. She
had accepted his decision, having no choice since
she couldn't force him to the altar, but she hadn't
forgiven him. It had been his love that hadn't been
strong enough, she realized. It had been his faith in
them that had been lacking, not hers. Now, looking
at his gentle smile, she felt only a great tenderness
toward him and something akin to pity.

She put his picture in her album. "My first love,"
she whispered, closing the cover. She lifted the
frame and kissed the spot over Roth's smiling face.
"My last love," she murmured.

For a moment longer, she thought of them: Tom,
who had said he loved her but wouldn't take what
life had offered; Roth, who didn't love her, but who
would take everything. And he had given, too, she
admitted. He had made her feel like a woman again.
His kisses had brought her back to painful, tingling

life again, and she would always be grateful for that. Companion, friend, lover—someday he would make some woman a wonderful husband.

Replacing the picture, she turned to the tasks at hand, unpacking her cases and planning the items she would need for the new job she was going to on Monday. She called her parents to let them know she was home, albeit temporarily.

Supper with Mrs. Wilkins brought her up to date on the neighborhood. She shared the recipes she had collected from Hattie and the chef at Sea Point and told her amusing stories of the two months in paradise. Finally, she said good night and went to her quarters.

Lying in bed, she reminded herself of several truths. Life does go on. Hearts can break, but they can also heal. Maybe she would fall in love again. Maybe next time they would both love equally. Maybe, she thought, maybe...

The lingering glow of twilight stretched across the sky of the May evening. Melba pulled her car into a parking space, turned off the ignition key, and hopped out. In the grocery, she quickly collected a few items to get her through the weekend.

A clerk in the meat department was removing cooked chickens from a machine that rotated them on a spit, baking them to an even gold all over. The aroma brought hunger pangs, so she added one of those to her cart.

The usual Friday evening melee of shoppers

crowded the aisles, and she moved patiently through them, her mind far away.

She had just got back to Charleston for the first time in three weeks, after staying with a patient near Summerville. The case had involved a young boy who had been in an accident. As well as taking care of his physical needs, she had helped him accept the fact that he would never be the football player he had planned to be. Another dream gone awry, she thought. But all in all, the treatment had been successful, and she had been pleased with his progress.

From her experiences with him and Adriane, she had decided she liked working with young people. She thought she would specialize in that age group. Pondering this future option, she picked up salad vegetables and a cantaloupe. Did she need anything else? Not that she could think of. She paid for the items and hurried to her car, suddenly anxious to get home.

Driving through the streets of Charleston, she nibbled on her lower lip. This weekend would, perhaps, mark a turning point in her own life. She had no assignment for two weeks.

If she picked up the phone and called Adriane and told her that she was coming to Webster Island to visit, would Roth be there, too? Did he still want her?

No one can guarantee the future. She realized that. She had been furious with Tom for refusing to take a chance, but she had been as uncertain with Roth. She had run out like a coward instead of trying to find out the depth of his feeling for her. Instead of that insouciant act she had put on, she should have been honest with him that last night. She had wanted commitment and caring from him. She should have told him that was how she felt toward him, even at the risk of being spurned.

Stopping in her driveway, she picked up her purse and the bag of groceries and went in the house, giving the front door a slam behind her. She started past the planter that divided the living room from the entrance area, then halted, unable to move another step.

Roth sat on the sofa. He gave her a rather solemn smile before placing the picture he had been studying on the end table. He came to her, his large hand catching the slipping bag as her fingers went numb with shock. His other arm encircled her waist, supporting her as her knees turned to water.

She stared, speechless, into his eyes, then she closed hers tightly. When she opened them, he was still there. "You're real," she said. Her fingers touched his cheek with the soft pat of a cat's paw.

"Yes," he assured her in the deeply vibrant baritone that she had heard only in her dreams for three weeks.

"Why are you here?" she asked, needing an explanation of this miracle which relieved her of the necessity of making that fateful decision to go to him.

"You left your sweater at Sea Point. I brought it to you." He looked at her gravely as he explained.

"Oh, thank you," she said in some confusion.

"You're welcome."

The conversation was ridiculous. She wanted to tell him a thousand things: how wonderful he looked, how glad she was to see him, how much she loved him. She scanned the teakwood hardness of his face and saw only tenderness. She gazed into his eyes and saw the fiery hunger. Yes, he still wanted her. That was one less uncertainty.

His smile touched his face lightly and was gone. He seemed hesitant, as if he were unsure of his welcome, and she experienced a need to reassure him.

"I'm glad to see you," she said.

"Are you?" he asked seriously, his eyes boring into hers. With an arm still around her, he led her into the kitchen. Quietly asking where things went, he helped her put away the groceries.

When the task was done, she sat in a chair at the table while he leaned against the counter. They smiled tentatively at each other, like young people on their first date. It was funny.

"Have you had dinner?" he asked, taking charge. She shook her head.

"Shall we go out?"

"No. There's a chicken that's cooked. I thought I would make a salad and slice the cantaloupe..." Her voice trailed off. Words seemed to have no meaning. The messages flashed between them silently. The air was electrified with them.

He nodded and turned to the task, preparing the meal she had suggested. Standing, she joined him, slicing the melon and putting water on to boil for tea. He added the tea leaves when the water was ready, setting the pan aside to steep. "This pitcher?" he asked.

"Yes," she said, amazed at how well they worked together. "How did you get in?" she remembered to ask him.

"Mrs. Wilkins. A very nice lady," he remarked. "She told me what a good tenant you are. No loud parties, no...men in and out at all hours. The pause before 'men' was hers."

Melba laughed softly, imagining the conversation.

"She offered to fix us a meal, but I told her we could manage."

"I see," Melba said.

He found plates and silver and set the table. Unwrapping the warm chicken, he placed it on a platter in the center of the table with the melon bowl next to it. She brought their salads over and then the iced-tea glasses, tinkling with ice cubes. Roth held her chair, neatly sliding it under her as she sat down. He took his place opposite her.

She ate silently while her thoughts went into turmoil. What was this all about? "How is Adriane?" she asked. "And Glenna and Hattie?"

"They're fine. They send their love."

So they knew he was here, she thought, swallowing past a lump in her throat. She listened carefully as he told her all the news of Webster and Hilton Head islands.

Greg and his family had left. The young man was going to college that summer to make up for the quarter he had missed while at Sea Point. He and Adriane were writing each other.

"I feel better with them having a long-distance romance," he confided.

"Over-protective," she accused. She cast a glance over the table and found his eyes on her, and her emotions went all topsy-turvy. He had confused and upset her from the moment they had met, she acknowledged.

"Glenna and Bruce have truly made up. They're spending the week at the island, and the place is so full of hearts and flowers, one can scarcely breathe. It's unnerving to come upon them in a clinch."

She laughed shakily at his dramatic grimace.

"It's gotten so bad, I'm afraid to go to my own house," he continued. "And it's all your fault."

"M-mine?"

"Y-yours," he confirmed, mimicking her stutter of stupefaction. He raised one dark brow in exasperation. "The place looks like a nudist colony. I'm sure we're going to be raided by the state police any day. Every time a plane flies over, I cringe, positive they've got us under surveillance. Probably taking pictures for evidence."

A puzzled expression appeared in her eyes. "But there's only Adriane and Glenna."

"And Bruce. And Hattie. Not at the same time, of course."

"Hattie! Surely she's not nude," she protested.

"Well, not yet," he conceded. "Adriane has gotten her into the pool and is teaching her to swim, and she is wearing a rather conservative one-piece suit at the present, but one wonders how long that will last,'' he said, his dry tone indicating he didn't think it would be much longer.

Again his descriptive word picture drew a laugh from her.

His deep chuckle joined hers. Looking at him, basking in his presence, delighting in his raillery, she knew without a doubt what she wanted. She wanted to be with him for however long he wanted her.

She had thought, listening to him tell Shirl how he felt, that she wouldn't be able to muster the poise the other woman had at the moment Roth definitely told her good bye; she would disgrace herself by crying, maybe clinging to him. She had thought the pain would be too great a price to pay.

But being away from him was worse. With him, she would know an exalting joy for a while. She would have that to off-set the loss when he was gone. And later, her heart would mend and she would survive. Looking at him, her eyes dark and stormy with her love, she knew this decision was the right one.

His tale of Webster Island continued. ''As for Bruce and Glenna, those two might be found in the pool at any hour of the day or night, cavorting like a pair of seals. It's damned embarrassing,'' he complained righteously. ''I mean, orgies in my own pool. I don't dare go out for my early morning swim anymore.''

Vividly, the vision of his lean body rising from the pool returned to her. She pressed a hand to her tummy.

The amusement left his face as he said softly, "We have you to thank for turning the island into a Garden of Eden."

"No, you're wrong," she said quickly.

He only looked at her, letting his eyes dispute her statement. Then he concentrated on his meal while she watched, waiting for him to finish. He polished off the remainder of the chicken and most of the melon before wiping his mouth, wadding the napkin into a ball and giving it a toss toward the wastebasket. It went in.

Like uncle, like niece, she thought, recalling Adriane doing the same thing the time she had been there. "Roth, why are you here?" She suddenly had to know, needing him to say the words.

The glow of his eyes burned a delicious path right to her insides. She felt heated and dizzy, as if the room were too warm.

"Come along," he ordered, his usual autocratic self once more. He guided her into the living room, pressing her into the corner of the sofa when they arrived. "Funny thing about lip prints," he commented, glancing at her. "They're like fingerprints, no two alike."

She was thoroughly mixed up by this bit of scientific fact. "Yes, that's true."

"Yes." He picked up the picture he had been viewing when she had arrived home. He held it this way and that, slanting it in the light of the lamp. "Glass reflects light from its surface at certain angles."

Sitting beside her, he held the picture so she could

see. When he angled it to the light, she could identify her lip prints on the glass, directly over Roth's face.

A slow blush spread over his face.

He replaced the frame on the low table. "Now. Another fact. I had an interesting talk with Nigel after you left last month." A strong hand reached out to turn her face to his. "He said you looked very upset when he met you in the lobby after you came out of the office. He talked to you to distract you, but he wondered what had happened, and he asked me if I knew. He was very concerned about you, as my whole family is."

Nigel had seen the unshed tears in her eyes, she realized. She lowered her lashes, unable to bear the keen scrutiny of Roth's eyes at this moment. An arm slipped around her shoulders, and she was pulled to his side.

"I had a rather embarrassing episode that evening, one that I had been unprepared for. That was my fault. I just didn't realize...well, anyway, I was waiting in my office for my date when another woman came in. She insisted she had to talk to me about something important. As soon as she started, I knew I needed to make her understand just what my intentions were concerning this other woman. You heard some of that conversation."

Melba nodded as he paused.

"What upset you?" he asked.

Could she tell him the truth? She had to try even if it meant exposing her deepest feelings to him. "Adriane had told me one time that once you were through with a woman, you were through forever. When I heard you tell Shirl, politely but firmly, that you wanted to be with me, it was obvious that you were telling her good-bye. She was very cool about it, but I knew I could never be that way. I...I...''

Roth lifted her hand and kissed the palm. ''You love me,'' he concluded. ''I was angry and hurt when you refused to come to me. I thought it meant that you didn't care. I thought I had read all the signs wrong. When you called my—'' he surprised her by turning slightly red ''—my courtship of you an interlude, I was furious. I had tried to be gentle and considerate and not take advantage of our mutual attraction, and then you hit me with that. I should have known you didn't mean it. I treated you badly, going off like that. Forgive me?''

He was so earnest that it melted her heart. ''Yes,'' she said. ''When I saw you here, I knew I wanted to be with you for as long as you want me.''

He made a small sound in his throat, and she felt his breath stop for a second. His arms tightened around her, pulling her to his chest. ''I checked with your office. You have two weeks off,'' he stated.

''Uh-huh,'' she murmured, closing her eyes in ecstasy and nestling her cheek against him.

''I called your parents. We're flying to Indiana tomorrow.''

She raised dazed eyes to his. ''To Indiana? Why?''

His hand tenderly cupped her face. ''To get married next weekend. We need to get the blood tests and all that done. And your parents will have a week to get to know their son-in-law. Adriane and her bunch will fly out for the wedding.''

She opened her mouth, then closed it. He had everything under control, and she had no objections to any of his plans.

He kissed her nose. "You haven't commented on the proposal," he reminded her.

A slow smile etched itself on her lips. "I haven't heard one yet."

"Will you? I love you very much—"

"Do you?" she interrupted. "That's the first time you've told me. When did you realize it?" she asked with a lover's curiosity about her loved one's thoughts.

"I told you before," he said.

She shook her head. "You've never mentioned love."

"Sure I did," he insisted. "That night in the kitchen when we had the cute little pony discussion, remember?"

"Of course, I do, but you didn't say anything about love."

He looked at her as if she were dense. "I chose you. I told you that. What else could it mean? And that night I got back from the trip—the night that you were with Nigel," he reminded her. "I told you then, too."

She sat up straight. "You did not!"

"I told you I had set my course for you...or something like that. Of course, I loved you. It was perfectly clear." He thought it over. Yes, he had definitely made his intentions known then.

Melba gave up the argument. "I thought you just wanted to have a summer fling with me."

He pulled her roughly into his arms. "Where did you get such a dumb idea? My family knew I was mad about you. They thought it hilarious that I was having to do all the running and getting nowhere. That was a new experience." He glanced at the picture on the table. "I know that Tom will always have a place in your heart. I'm not jealous, not if I have a place, too."

He was so humble, it broke her heart into pieces. "A memory is only a small thing. It has its own place," she told him. "You have my entire heart. All of it. All of me."

Her look was one of pure adoration, spilling over him like a crashing wave from her stormy sea-green eyes. Her fingers stroked his cheek, and he caught her hand and brought it to her lips. That wasn't enough. In the next instant, she was crushed in a viselike grip. He laughed exultantly, happily.

"We'll get a place here in town," he planned while his hands roamed over her, exploring his treasure. "Can you handle only day cases from now on? I'd like to have you with me at night. Otherwise, your patients will have to accept me as part of the package." He grinned wickedly at her, bringing a laugh to her lips.

He pulled her knit shirt off over her head and unfastened her bra, tossing both items behind the sofa. "Ah, my very own flaming dessert," he murmured. "Crisp like toast, sweet like peaches," he teased her as he had the first time they had met.

"I've loved you almost from the first moment I saw you. Adriane had been singing your praises for weeks, and I was intrigued by this paragon who could win her respect so completely. Then to discover that you were also the nymph who had been hiding on the patio...it had to mean something special."

"I felt closer to Adriane than any patient I ever had," she told him. "I was afraid of you, though. You made me feel so many conflicting emotions. I thought it was only the reawakening of passion, but that day when Bruce came over to the island with you, then I couldn't hide the truth from myself any longer. I loved you."

He took her face between his hands and stamped a trail of burning kisses all over it. "We'll honeymoon on Webster and Sunrise islands. I've given everybody orders to vacate by next Saturday." He lifted her in his strong arms, walking confidently toward her bedroom.

"Sunrise Island?" she asked, putting her arms around him and leaving her own path of kisses along his neck.

"It's a tagalong island next to Webster. We'll have picnics there. And every dawn, we'll watch the sun rise over the sea," he told her huskily.

She pressed her face into the curve of his neck, her heart filled with love for him. In her bedroom, he laid her on the bed, then his hands moved competently over her as he removed the rest of her clothing. She rolled to her side and watched him as he undressed. His shirt hit the floor, then his shoes and socks followed. In a minute, he stood before her, strongly masculine and unabashedly aroused.

Even as she admired his tanned, healthy body, her mind roamed over many facets of her feelings for him. Adriane had been correct in her assessment of her favorite relative. Roth was not a user of people. He was a man of deep emotions—love, compassion, and integrity—and he had shown all of those to Melba in his concern for Adriane as well as his treatment of herself.

He sat on the side of the bed, and his hand stroked slowly along her ribs and abdomen in a caress that was at once passionate and soothing. He was a man of understanding, his touch gentle on her as he began the ritual of becoming her lover.

"You're everything I want, everything I've ever dreamed of in a woman," he said. His hand cupped her breast. "I'll be glad to see our child in your arms, suckling here at your breast." He was still for a moment, just looking at her. Then, "It will be the physical symbol of our love, our continuity with time, our future. I thought of all that when I saw you."

Tears filled her eyes. "Oh, Roth. Oh, love," she whispered, aching with love for him.

His hand slipped down to her abdomen. His fingers pressed the flat wall of muscle there as he thought of the child she would carry. He took a deep breath. "I would never willingly hurt you. But I'll never give you up," he added fiercely. "Not for your own good, not for mine, not for anything!"

She raised up and hugged him to her, their bare

skin merging in points of fire. "Nor me. I've been so unhappy without you."

"These past weeks have been hell," he agreed, his lips moving softly along her neck. With a sudden shift, he stretched out beside her, pressing her body with his, his leg seeking the warm enclosure of her thighs.

She clasped his thigh between hers, her hands running all over her dynamic lover in increasing demands as she gave free rein to the desire that burned in her. He responded to her touch as she did to his. They smiled into each other's eyes.

"You knew from the first," she whispered. "How?"

"I don't know," he said, sweeping his hand along her side, to her thigh and back to her luscious breast. "I only know I've never cared for a woman the way I care for you. You were so lovely, and yet, so emotionally on guard. I had to find the person you had hidden behind that efficient facade. I saw the way you related to Adriane. I saw your innate tenderness and I knew I had to have you for myself. My woman. My gift from the gods." His grin was slightly crooked as he lowered his mouth toward hers. "I made a spectacle of myself over you, you obtuse ninny," he teased in the way that only he had. "You owe me for that."

His tongue drew a damp circle at the corner of her mouth. "I'll sigh over you in front of my family," she promised.

"You'd better." His mouth closed over hers, and words were forgotten. His tongue tasted her mouth for endless moments of joy. She was so perfect. Every part of her body that he explored was flawless in its design.

She gave herself to the fantasy of loving him as she had dreamed of doing. His citrus-scented after-shave mixed with the perfume of their entwined bodies. She was aware of him in every nerve ending in her body, with all her senses.

His hands were gentle as they roamed over her, bringing her to higher and higher peaks of desire. Passion so sweet it was almost painful, flowed like a mighty sea between them. He pressed for the ultimate contact, and she awakened beneath his touch as if she were the earth and he were the life-giving sun.

Together, they merged their destinies into one, and it was all either of them had ever dreamed.

"Yes," she said, holding on to him, trying to answer every kiss of his with one of her own. His mouth was possessive and ardent.

"Your perfume is like wildflowers," he said. "I could make love to you forever." He talked to her as his hands excited her to bliss, his words flowing into her and filling her with his love and his passion.

And when she could hold no more, when she was overflowing, he held her and let her love pour over him until she was drained and empty and utterly content. And then he led her to the well of his endless love and filled her again.

They slept, at peace in the world of their new love. At the first light, they woke, turning instinctively to each other.

"I had a dream once at Webster," she told him. "You were in it and so was Tom. He looked so sad. You beckoned me to come to you. I think my heart was trying to tell me then that Tom was the past and you were my future." She touched his face with a caressing hand as if to make sure he wasn't still part of a dream.

Roth lifted his head from where he was nuzzling her breast. "I'm not jealous," he said, "but if you mention another man's name while I'm making love to you ever again, I'm going to choke you." He gave her a stern look, then his face softened into a smile of love.

"I'm sorry," she said contritely.

He bit her neck, then nibbled at her mouth. His body rose over hers, inciting her with wanton desire as his knee slipped between her thighs. He claimed her for himself, imprinting his love on her memory as he had promised, so that she was aware of only him. Together they found the ecstasy that comes with the joining of heart and mind and soul.

"Look," Roth said later, as they rested in the sweet afterglow. He nodded toward the window. Lying in each other's arms, they watched the sky brighten until it seemed the earth trembled in anticipation of the event. And then the golden sphere rose over the horizon.

"Sunrise," she said quietly. "It seems as if it's the very first day."

He pulled her closer. "For us, it is."

*   *   *   *   *

Silhouette
SPECIAL EDITION™®

SPECIAL EDITION

Stories of love and life, these powerful
novels are tales that you can identify with—
romances with "something special" added
in!

Fall in love with the stories of authors such
as **Nora Roberts, Diana Palmer, Ginna Gray**
and many more of your special favorites—as
well as wonderful new voices!

Special Edition brings you
entertainment for the heart!

SSE-GEN

WAYS TO UNEXPECTEDLY MEET MR. RIGHT:

♡ *Go out with the sexy-sounding stranger your daughter secretly set you up with through a personal ad.*

♡ *RSVP yes to a wedding invitation—soon it might be your turn to say "I do!"*

♡ *Receive a marriage proposal by mail— from a man you've never met....*

These are just a few of the unexpected ways that written communication leads to love in Silhouette Yours Truly.

Each month, look for two fast-paced, fun and flirtatious Yours Truly novels (with entertaining treats and sneak previews in the back pages) by some of your favorite authors—and some who are sure to become favorites.

YOURS TRULY™:
Love—when you least expect it!

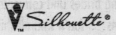

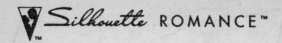

What's a single dad to do when he needs a wife by next Thursday?

Who's a confirmed bachelor to call when he finds a baby on his doorstep?

How does a plain Jane in love with her gorgeous boss get him to notice her?

From classic love stories to romantic comedies to emotional heart tuggers, **Silhouette Romance** offers six irresistible novels every month by some of your favorite authors! Such as…beloved bestsellers **Diana Palmer, Annette Broadrick, Suzanne Carey, Elizabeth August** and **Marie Ferrarella,** to name just a few—and some sure to become favorites!

Fabulous Fathers…Bundles of Joy…Miniseries… Months of blushing brides and convenient weddings… Holiday celebrations… You'll find all this and much more in **Silhouette Romance**—always emotional, always enjoyable, always about love!

If you've got the time...
We've got the
INTIMATE MOMENTS

Passion. Suspense. Desire. Drama. Enter a world that's larger than life, where men and women overcome life's greatest odds for the ultimate prize: love. Nonstop excitement is closer than you think...in Silhouette Intimate Moments!

SIM-GEN

Do you want...

Dangerously handsome heroes

Evocative, everlasting love stories

Sizzling and tantalizing sensuality

Incredibly sexy miniseries like **MAN OF THE MONTH**

Red-hot romance

Enticing entertainment that can't be beat!

You'll find all of this, and much *more* each and every month in **SILHOUETTE DESIRE**. Don't miss these unforgettable love stories by some of romance's hottest authors. Silhouette Desire—where your fantasies will always come true....